I0667940

SIX-GUN ACTION!

Longarm swept the waiting-room crowd for some Texas law. He didn't see any. He took a deep breath, turned around, and drew his .44-40. There was just no better way to take even one of them alive, and dead men tell no tales about who'd hired them. So he strode back into the bar, gun leveled, in hopes he'd gotten the drop on them.

It didn't work. Longarm would never know what he'd done to make the older gunslick spook. He only knew that when he came back in they were both facing his way, and the older one had already gone for his gun.

Nobody fooled around with a .44 double-action, so Longarm shot to kill, downing his man with a plain old .44-40 over the heart. But the younger gunslick had his own iron in hand—and the barrel sighted in on Deputy Marshal Long . . .

DISCARDED

DON'T MISS THESE
ALL-ACTION WESTERN SERIES
FROM THE BERKLEY PUBLISHING GROUP

THE GUNSMITH by J. R. Roberts
Clint Adams was a legend among lawmen, outlaws, and ladies. They called him . . . the Gunsmith.

LONGARM by Tabor Evans
The popular long-running series about U.S. Deputy Marshal Long—his life, his loves, his fight for justice.

LONE STAR by Wesley Ellis
The blazing adventures of Jessica Starbuck and the martial arts master, Ki. Over eight million copies in print.

SLOCUM by Jake Logan
Today's longest-running action Western. John Slocum rides a deadly trail of hot blood and cold steel.

TABOR EVANS

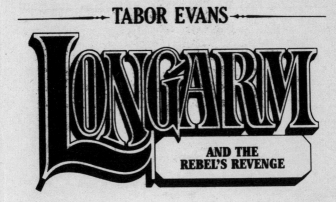

LONGARM

AND THE
REBEL'S REVENGE

JOVE BOOKS, NEW YORK

If you purchased this book without a cover, you should be aware that this book is stolen property. It was reported as "unsold and destroyed" to the publisher, and neither the author nor the publisher has received any payment for this "stripped book."

LONGARM AND THE REBEL'S REVENGE

A Jove Book / published by arrangement with
the author

PRINTING HISTORY
Jove edition / November 1993

All rights reserved.
Copyright © 1993 by Jove Publications, Inc.
This book may not be reproduced in whole
or in part, by mimeograph or any other means,
without permission. For information address:
The Berkley Publishing Group, 200 Madison Avenue,
New York, New York 10016.

ISBN: 0-515-11238-0

A JOVE BOOK®
Jove Books are published by The Berkley Publishing Group,
200 Madison Avenue, New York, New York 10016.
JOVE and the "J" design
are trademarks belonging to Jove Publications, Inc.

PRINTED IN THE UNITED STATES OF AMERICA

10 9 8 7 6 5 4 3 2 1

MANITOUWADGE PUBLIC LIBRARY

00021995

LONGARM

AND THE
REBEL'S REVENGE

MANITOUWADGE PUBLIC LIBRARY

Chapter 1

The trouble with killing folks was that no excuse was ever going to be enough for all their kith and kin. If you shot a syphilitic maniac as he was ravaging his own child, in church, some sorehead was sure to opine you should have understood a man has needs.

So U.S. Deputy Marshal Custis Long had gotten heaps of letters such as this one in the six or eight years he'd been riding with a badge for Uncle Sam. But this one seemed just silly and he said so.

He was seated at the time in the oak-paneled inner office of his boss, Marshal Billy Vail of the Denver District Court. The somewhat older and far stubbier superior behind the cluttered desk blew yet another tumbleweed of pungent cigar smoke at the scoffer and said, "The first one was postmarked San Antone. That one you find so amusing was sent from El Paso. I got one here postmarked in Santa Fe. You want to read it?"

Longarm, as he was better known to friend and foe alike, got out a three-for-a-nickel cheroot in self-defense as he replied, "Not if it don't say something more original. Anyone can see the sender is out to spook the senator by sending each death threat a good ways closer to the Colorado State House. That don't mean anyone's really out to assassinate a state senator to avenge the dumb death of some enemy soldier he killed fair and square in the damn war. And way back in the greenup of '62!"

Vail nodded. "That does seem quite a spell to hold a grudge. But Texicans are good at holding grudges, and the Colorado Firsters did give Sibley's West Texas Brigade a good shellacking at Glorieta Pass, you know."

Longarm said without regret, "I missed out on that fun, being sort of busy at the time at another place called Shiloh, but those Colorado Firster vets who hang out at the Parthenon Saloon sure do like to talk about it. So I'll agree it was a bitter hard-scrabble fight betwixt glorified guerrilla bands, if you'll agree nobody with a lick of sense could single out one trooper riding with the First Colorado Volunteers who'd dropped one particular boy in butternut with that big West Texas raiding column. To hear old-timers at the Parthenon tell it, Colonel John Slough moved out from Fort Union with better than thirteen hundred volunteers, aiming to take on Confederate Colonel Sibley at the head of thirty-seven hundred out of West Texas and bound for the Pikes Peak gold fields. Slough must have been *loco en la cabeza*."

Vail shrugged, blew more smoke, and said, "He won, didn't he? A Johnny Reb loaded for bear on his own cow pony in a butternut shirt his true love sewed for him is one thing. Even a part-time volunteer militiaman is another, trained by regulars and equipped by the U.S. Army Quartermaster Corps. Like I said, the Firsters won big, in a campaign that cost both sides dearly. So your point about singling out a particular death by gunfire is well taken. Sibley's West Texas brigade is estimated to have lost six or eight hundred riders in the dusty hills of New Mexico Territory before he made his famous run for home. I say *estimated* because Confederate record-keeping was a sometimes thing, even in their more regular outfits. As you may have heard at the Parthenon around the April anniversary of Glorieta, the Gettysburg of the

West, the whupped and running Texicans left their dead and wounded scattered from Hell to breakfast betwixt Pigeon Ranch and Santa Fe. But the writer of the death threat in your hand says it was his dear old dad that a then-way-younger Senator J. Jennings Fraser murdered dirty somewhere along the way."

Longarm lit his own smoke and searched in vain for an ashtray for his smoldering match as he remarked, "And the letter says he, she, or it has now grown old enough to *do* something about it. What do you reckon the sender means by Trooper Fraser shooting Dear Old Dad deliberately? I hardly saw anyone get shot *accidentally* in that war."

Vail looked uncomfortable and suggested, "It has been said that the brawl betwixt undisciplined militia got a mite ugly at times. You must have heard by now how old John Chivington, the militant minister, bayonetted Confederate supply mules at Apache Canyon as one of Slough's battalion leaders at the time."

It had been more a statement than a question, but Longarm nodded as he ground out the waterproof wax match on Vail's carpet, replying, "Colorado vets brag about Glorieta Pass to the point of tedious. But it's almost impossible to find any who'll own up to riding under the same Butcher Chivington at Sand Creek."

Vail nodded. "That was sure a shitty way to treat women and children, even if they was Cheyenne. Why did you just grind a damned Mex match into my carpet, old son?"

Longarm replied, "I carry 'em because they're waterproof, not because they go out easy. It's your own fault for not having anything but this one damned chair on this side of your desk. I ain't about to put a smoldering wax match in the pockets of this tweed frock coat you make me wear around this Federal Building. Now getting back to what I might be doing here, they do say Chivington ordered his men to hang some captured rebel scouts because he thought they were out of uniform."

3

Vail nodded. "He was that sort of soldier, when he wasn't preaching the gospel at First Methodist. But these letters all accuse State Senator Fraser, not the Reverend Colonel Chivington, of wrongfully *shooting* Dear Old Dad, not *hanging* him. In either event, I want you to mosey up Capitol Hill to the State House, report to Senator Fraser, and tell him our answer to the nasty letters he's been getting of late. Don't you dare flick them ashes on my carpet on your way out!"

Longarm didn't, even though it smarted to drop them in the palm of his other hand as he mildy asked, "How come it's our chore, Boss? Ain't Colorado got no state police these days?"

Vail said, "The senator requested the help of the U.S. Justice Department, for reasons I'm too modest to brag about, and he rates it because he's an elected official up for a third term and killing him or even threatening to kill him can't be constitutional."

Longarm said that was good enough for him, and left before he had to burn his hand with more hot ashes. He naturally dumped his load, and flicked more ash after it, when he made it out to the front office. The young squirt who played the typewriter and told visitors they need an appointment to see Marshal Vail protested, "Damn it, you careless moose, I have to sweep up out here!"

Longarm nodded amiably. "I know, Henry. But seeing you got to anyway, ain't it nice to know you won't be sweeping in vain?"

He left as Henry was saying something mighty pungent for such a prissy-looking young cuss, and went down a tedious number of stone steps, inside and out, till he was striding east toward the oddly named Broadway of downtown Denver.

Seventeenth Street, running east and west a few blocks over to Longarm's right, was the closest thing to a main street Denver had. It ran from the Union Depot straight to where it took one hell of turn at Broadway to run up

4

Capitol Hill, which was really more the west rim of the High Plains where they dropped down to the flats where Cherry Creek met the South Platte to flood downtown Denver whenever it got to really raining.

Broadway ran along the apron of the long rise at about a thirty-odd-degree angle to the downtown grid. Despite its name, Broadway served more to separate the business district from more refined notions such as churches, schools, state government installations, and high-priced houses. Longarm and others living on honest wages got to live on the less fashionable side of Cherry Creek to the southwest, clean across the South Platte where the plains rose again to be described less elegantly as Irish Hill, Little Palestine, or whatever, depending on the writing above the neighborhood store-fronts.

Catching sight of himself in a fancier store-front as he strode across Broadway, Longram was glad he'd had his telescoped Stetson mended, steamed, and blocked since that last shootout. His store-bought three-piece suit of almost matching tobacco brown tweed had been cleaned and pressed more recently than he'd last rolled in horseshit while dressed for the office. He paused near the plate glass to get his shoestring tie straighter. If they wanted him to tote his old .44-40 Colt Double Action any differently it was too damned bad. The new dress regulations of the Hayes reform Administration didn't call for a man getting shot just because he was a federal employee, and a lawman who didn't pack his sidearm sensibly in a cross-draw rig with the grips riding handy under an infernal frock coat was a lawman who might not be long for this wicked world.

Satisfied he looked sissy enough for the State House, he swung southeast along Broadway to where it met the terraced, sheep-sheared, Capitol grounds, and swung up Colfax Avenue toward the State House dominating the skyline to the east. Halfway up the tree-shaded thoroughfare Longarm took advantage of a passing clanging horse-drawn streetcar to whip around behind a sturdy tree trunk for a sudden study of the slate-flagged walk behind him. The same good old tree trunk still packed a bullet meant for Longarm's back on an earlier occasion. A guilty conscience could have that effect on a moody crook viewing a well-known lawman headed for where a heap of laws got started. But that morning nobody was on the walk except two ladies headed down toward Broadway.

Words inscribed on the third granite step of the side entrance to the State House bragged that it stood exactly one mile above mean sea level. Longarm had already known that. He stode on up into the scaled-down answer to the less gray Capitol Building in Washington, and found his way to Senator Fraser's office suite near the marble-floored rotunda. A pretty but sort of sour-faced secretary inside told him the senator was in the senate chamber down the hall doing something about silver. They were always doing something about silver in Colorado. They mined one hell of a lot of it along the Front Range, where the senator ran for office every four years. Senators from the parts where they mined a heap of gold were always trying to do something else about the ratio of gold to silver prices on the market. Longarm didn't care. He had neither a gold nor silver mine to call his own, and they paid him the same modest wages no matter how rich sports like Silver Dollar Tabor or Leadville Johnny Brown might wind up.

He told the sour-faced secretary who he was, and explained he'd been sent to look into those grim letters they'd been getting. From the blank look in the big blue eyes above the lemon-sucking mouth he decided she was either awfully stupid or awfully smart. He nodded and said he'd best take the personal matter up with her boss.

Colorado, like most states, had a bicameral setup with a senate meeting in one wing and a house of representatives down the other way. They only held joint sessions every other winter. It was tough to say what they thought they were doing the rest of the time.

Longarm knew the doors to the senate chamber would be barred on the main floor. So he went upstairs, where an open and unguarded door led into the public gallery, a narrow balcony overlooking all the bald heads and cigar smoke doing something about silver.

Some old windbag had the floor. He was either making a speech or telling jokes, from the way other windbags kept laughing at him. It was tough to tell when an old boy used long words he didn't understand through poorly fitting false teeth.

The public gallery was almost deserted, since so few cared any more than Longarm about the fortunes of the Colorado mining moguls. A couple in their teens was down at one far end, in the back row, carrying on in a way that hinted that the young gal's folks likely watched her tighter on their front porch.

The only adults there before him seemed to be a sporty-dressed squirt who looked like a ladies' hairdresser on his day off and a lady in a downright ridiculous hat. She was in an aisle seat just down from the door. The gallery sloped considerably. Longarm move on down to sit across the aisle from her, lest she take him for snooty or forward. He spotted the silver hair of Senator Fraser down at a desk Longarm could have hit with a wad of spit easily from where he sat. It hardly made one feel comfortable with those repeated death threats. One of the first moves he meant to make would be to position at least two good men, like Deputies Smiley and Dutch, up here with their Winchesters.

Since the senator seemed safe from assassination at the moment, Longarm caught himself admiring the cameo profile under that dumb hat. He suspected a pretty gal that young had to have borrowed the hat from some older, richer, dowdier relation. It looked as if they were trying for a tossed salad of artificial flowers and dead birds, all the same autumn shades. And the well-filled watered-silk bodice that slithered down her swell front from a choke collar was the warm brown of an autumn oak leaf. It made her upswept chestnut hair seem a tad more coppery, so likely she'd picked out the whole outfit. She'd had money to spend on it, and that hat didn't seem quite as dumb once a man studied more on what was under it.

The sport in the dapper suit and small pimp mustache under a cocky porkpie hat must have been studying the same cameo profile from the far side. For he was suddenly looming over her, hat in hand, to offer her a violet mint from the small paper bag he no doubt carried at all times for such emergencies.

The lady in the funny hat, being a lady, naturally ignored him. He sat down beside her anyway, protesting that he only wanted to be her protector in the wild and wicked city.

Longarm knew better. But the cameo profile was getting pinker by the minute as she pretended to be paying rapt attention to that old windbag down below. So Longarm rose to his considerable height, moved up one step to work in behind them, and tapped the sport on the shoulder hard. "I believe you're in my seat, friend."

The sport turned with a look intended to be tough, till he saw who he was up against. Then his voice seemed less certain. "Oh? Do you know this lady, cowboy?"

Longarm gripped the sport's collarbone tight as he smiled in a wolfish way and said, "We went to school together. Would you like to quit while you're ahead, or would you care to have me show you how I punch cows?"

The sport said, "Hey, let's not have a hoedown over this little—" Longarm's steely fingers bit into him in a more warning way. "*Lady!*" the sport finished. So Longarm let him go and, naturally, he went.

As soon as the seat next to the gal was vacated, Longarm swung his long legs over the seat-back and sat down beside her, removing his Stetson as he murmured, "Pay me no mind and nobody else will pester you now, ma'am."

But she turned to him with a weary smile and murmured

8

back, "Thank you, sir. But do we have to put up with that *other* silly behavior?"

"I'm afraid so, ma'am. They always carry on that way down yonder. Folks with delicate feelings should never watch sausages being made or laws enacted."

"I didn't mean down *there*." She turned away, blushing even more. So Longarm took a closer look at what the young couple was up to, or down on, at the far end.

He called out, not unkindly, "Cut that out and take her on up to the less crowded balcony inside the dome, old son. You'll find the small door marked No Admittance will admit you to considerable dark privacy betwixt the inner and outer domes."

They pretended not to hear him. They were likely about to come. He said, "I mean it, and I'm the law, if you'd rather take this up with your homefolk."

It worked. After they'd left, blushing beet red as they buttoned up on the way out, the lady next to Longarm, pretending not to see, murmured, "Thank you again. I might have known you were a lawman. I was wondering what a sensible well-behaved gentleman might be doing up here at this hour with such a tiresome bill before the senate."

He put his hat back on, observing, "You look sensible yourself, no offense. And you ain't been misbehaving far as I can tell, ma'am."

She demurely replied, "I'm waiting for my guardian, Senator J. Jennings Fraser. I'm Kate Thayer, and you must be the detective the U.S. marshal promised to send over."

He told her his name and added, "I ain't exactly what you'd call a detective, Miss Kate. I'm only a deputy marshal. I know just a mite about detecting, but first I got to figure what we seem to be jawing about. I was just down to the senator's office. I got the impression he might not have told his office staff about the death threats."

She nodded—it did alarming things to the tossed sal-

9

ad atop her head—and explained, "My guardian doesn't know just whom we want to trust with such uncertain matters. He asked for federal help because he suspects political enemies may be behind the silly threats and while he'd hardly have political rivals at the federal level, his Colorado enemies have spies everywhere!"

Longarm didn't think it would be polite to ask, and he didn't expect her to know, whether the senator saw spooky shapes in his bedchamber after dark. Those notes Billy Vail had in his office, sent via the U.S. mails, were at least as real as odd shadows looming in a corner after sundown. So he asked why she kept calling the senator her guardian.

He was almost sorry he'd asked as Kate Thayer went into a tale of almost tedious woe. He found her company pleasant and her voice enjoyable in its high-toned way. But Billy Vail hadn't sent him to guard the life of a dead mining magnate's full-grown but somewhat reckless-sounding daughter.

Since most folk would, he figured she was sort of playing down the parts about her running off from that finishing school with a self-styled French baron who'd turned out to be a fortune hunter.

She admitted her widowed daddy had been right about the cuss when old Marcel, as he'd been called, had taken the payoff and let the family lawyer, J. Jennings Fraser, have the marriage of a runaway in her teens annulled. He hadn't been elected a state senator yet at the time. Since Colorado senate terms ran four years, and the silver-haired old bird had already served close to three full terms, Kate Thayer had to be closer to Longarm's own age than she looked.

As if she'd read his mind, she explained, "I don't think my poor father trusted some of the other gentleman callers I may have had in the years he had left. No matter how many times I assured him I'd more than learned my lesson, he left my rather handsome inheritance in trust with his lawyer, now Senator Fraser, as trustee. I was well over twenty-one, alas, when my father was crushed to death in one of our stamping mills. But I don't get the capital or bulk of the estate with power to run the family firm until I'm forty."

She looked away as she added wistfully, "I suppose Father felt any man who came courting an old maid would have to be sincere. In the meantime Senator Fraser sees to my father's mines and mills and I'm allowed a generous income without having to concern myself about taxes *or* the ratio between gold and silver prices."

"Which do you mine and process?" Longarm asked without really caring as another man came in to take a seat near where those fool kids had been fooling with each other's privates. The cuss was in his late thirties or early forties, dressed sort of like an undertaker might dress on his day off, if the undertaker was packing a gun in that odd bulge under the left shoulder.

Not wanting to let the stranger suspect he was being watched with that much interest, Longarm told the gal beside him, "Lucky for you the letters have all come from out of town so far. I know *I'd* surely hate an old cuss I wasn't even kin to doling out my daddy's dollars as he might see fit!"

She sighed. "There have been times I've resented the senator. I wanted my own private railroad car when I was younger, and I couldn't see why I couldn't have one if that stuck-up Augusta Tabor got to ride about in one. But of course, as I've grown older and hopefully wiser, I've come to understand why my father intended for me to live, and quite well, on no more than the share of the firm's profits that my legal guardian passes on to me. As for that remark about death threats, I could have the senator murdered right this instant and it wouldn't change a thing. He let me see the books as well as all the papers when I confronted him about being a mean old thing some years ago. He proved to my satisfaction that

11

I've been getting a little more than my father planned for. The senator got the probate court to allow for the higher prices since the big depression of the seventies. As for his dying before I come of an age to take full charge of my financial affairs, my father covered that in his will. The estate was entrusted to the senator's law firm rather than to any particular partner. There are close to a dozen all told. When or if the senior partner dies or chooses to retire, my estate will be probated for administration to the new senior partner. Frankly, I find it easier to get along with my father's old war comrade and lawyer than some of the younger partners he's taken on since he got so big."

That tall dark drink of water was reaching under his rusty black frock coat now, and his jaw dropped considerably when he found himself staring into the unwinking muzzle of Longarm's .44–40.

He gaped at the tall tweed-suited stranger now looming over him at point-blank range, and marveled, "Do you always move that sudden, Uncle Sam?"

Longarm softly answered, "Only when I have to. Haul that hand out slow and empty, friend."

As the stranger did so Kate Thayer rose to head on over, wide-eyed, asking, "Why are you pointing a gun at the gentleman, Custis?"

Longarm said, "I'll know better after he tells me how come he was going for his shoulder holster, and how he knew I was federal."

The seated man staring up at them smiled wanly and said, "I was only going for a smoke. I pack my cigars in an inside breast pocket. Come to consider, that *is* sort of close to my shoulder rig. I knew who you were because you've been pointed out to me on the street as someone never to mess with. Miss Kate here can tell you who I am."

Longarm kept the mysterious stranger covered as he shot a puzzled glance at the well-proportioned gal in autumn brown silk. She dimpled up at him and said,

12

"Custis, this is Detective Durante from that Pinkerton Agency. I hired him from my own allowance when those death threats started coming."

The Pinkerton man explained, "I was out in the hall, keeping my own eyes open, when you started chasing folks out of here. I came in to make sure you were really who I'd thought I saw come in here. Besides, like I said, I wanted a smoke."

Longarm put his gun away and suggested they all sit down. As they did so he addressed the pretty heiress. "Does the senator know about this? And how come *you* know so much, Miss Kate, if the man the death threats were addressed to never saw fit to tell his own sour-faced secretary?"

Kate Thayer smiled faintly. "You're right about the poor thing's unfortunate expression. I didn't know whether the senator had told her about the unpleasant mail. He may or may not have told any particular member of his own law firm. You'll have to ask him. He only told me when I confronted him with one of the odd letters addressed to *me*."

Longarm frowned. "They've been sending death threats to you as well, Miss Kate?"

She shook her head, an amazing display of tossed salad, and told him, "I imagine I don't qualify, since I'd have been a kid in pigtails at the time. But they must have wanted me to know about it. Do you have that typed copy of that last grotesque letter, Detective Durante?"

The Pinkerton man raised the flap of his frock coat wide to let Longarm see he was after some paper in an inside breast pocket as he assured his lady boss he surely did.

He took out the folded bond paper and handed it to Longarm, saying, "Between you and me, Uncle Sam, I suspect we're dealing with a harmless crank. I've said as much to Miss Kate here, but it's her money and she who pays the piper calls the tune."

Longarm took the paper with a nod of thanks and

13

unfolded it. He got just enough light from the brighter senate chamber to make out the message addressed to Kate at her fancy Denver townhouse. It said:

"You think your guardian, Senator Fraser, is so grand. But let me tell you a tale of his brilliant military career with the First Colorado, down betwixt Apache Canyon and Glorieta Pass, when he was riding with Butcher Chivington's bloody battalion!"

Longarm paused to ask, "How could the writer know anybody in any blamed battalion had become your father's lawyer? You say your father was in the war too?"

She nodded. "Wasn't everybody who was old enough to serve at the time? My father wasn't in the same battalion, but he rode with the Colorado Firsters and my mother had a fit about it. Both he and Lawyer Fraser were old enough to avoid the draft without joining the part-time militia."

Longarm nodded. "Neither side resorted to conscription for over a year after the battle of Glorieta, and even then a married man with kids was allowed to hire a substitute to go in his place."

He read on. "Like yourself, I was too young at the time to serve our own cause. But my father, like your father and that murdering cowardly toad named J.J. Fraser, rode to battle in the Sangre de Cristo country of New Mexico."

The old windbag who had the floor below seemed to have run out of wind. So another old windbag was moving they adjourn till after noon dinner. They were debating how long it might take to drink a noon dinner as Longarm read on.

"Your father and mine doubtless felt they were fighting for a just cause, and since both fought honorably, I'll say no more about anyone else there on either side. My father was serving honorably as a Confederate scout when he was captured, in uniform, no matter how shabby his butternut shirt and gray sombrero may have seemed to part-time soldiers in fancy Union blue. Butcher Chivington told my father and his brave comrades they could tell him where

14

the rest of their Texas column was or be shot on the spot as irregulars. Needless to say, my father and his brave comrades refused. It was the cowardly Senator Fraser, a lance corporal at the time, who carried out his bloodthirsty commander's orders when, and only when, all the other officers and noncommissioned officers there refused on the grounds of simple military justice!"

Downstairs, someone was pounding a gavel to turn all the thirsty if not famished lawmakers loose as Longarm read on. "My father and the other members of this patrol were forced to dig their own graves in the hard adobe soil. Then they were shot, one by one, at the nape of the neck, by J.J. Fraser and no others as they knelt by the edge of their mass grave. It was years before their families learned the horrid details of their final fate, and more years before I was in any position to do anything about it."

Longarm heard a commotion in the second-story hall-way outside as he read on. "Need I explain all the steps I intend to take now that I am on my way to Colorado at last? Since I bear the daughter of a more honorable enemy no ill will, I strongly advise you to stay well clear of our gallant Senator Fraser for the short time he has left to sully this world with his protracted existence in it!"

The curious favor to a lady hadn't been signed with so much as an X. Before Longarm could ask if that had been the case with the original letter, the silver-haired Senator Fraser came in from the hall with an apologetic smile. "Sorry to keep you waiting so long for the lunch I promised you, Kathleen."

Then he saw the two men who seemed to be with her, and paused with an uncertain smile. He went on smiling as he heard who Longarm was. But when Kate introduced the Pinkerton man, and allowed that she'd hired him, the trustee who doled out her allowance favored her with one of those looks parents reserve for cute children with dirty faces. "It was supposed to be a secret, and you know what Good Queen Bess said about two being able to keep a secret as long as one of them was dead!"

Longarm said, "I read somewheres it was Machiavelli, and the one who wrote letters to two or more people doubtless knows about 'em, sir. I can vouch for the Pinkerton Agency being honest by the standards old Boss Cameron of Philadelphia set for his machine politicians."

Kate Thayer looked blank as Detective Durante said, "Thanks, I think."

The senator smiled dryly and intoned, "An honest politician is a man who stays bought. We insist on as much from members of our Colorado machine. But I still wish my sweet young ward would quit trying to help. When she came to me with her own crank letters I told her I'd handle it myself. Besides, Marshal Vail sent somebody, didn't he?"

Longarm nodded. "That's about the size of it. But if I were you folks I'd keep the Pinks now that you've retained them. As I said, they've a rep for staying loyal as long as they're working for you. But your point's well taken about keeping the list of our possible suspects down. So far it's yet to appear in the *Denver Post,* and Detective Durante can explain detecting guilty knowledge if he'd like to."

Durante said he'd like no such thing, adding, "Any fool can see how only the letter writer and those let in on the letters ought to be at all interested in the Battle of Glorieta at this late date."

So the senator agreed, and asked what Longarm thought they ought to do next.

To which Longarm could only reply, "Let's go eat. I only had a couple of eggs over chili con carne for breakfast and I'm just about faint with starvation!"

Chapter 2

They had a fancy dining room smack in the State House, but at Longarm's suggestion the four of them traipsed over to a place he knew about near the Papist cathedral atop Capitol Hill. It was clean and fancy enough for priests and nuns to eat in. More important, nobody gunning for a state senator had good cause to lay for him there instead of the State House dining room.

Not knowing who was paying, Longarm said he'd never been sick on their usual specials of the day. But Kate Thayer still ordered a fresh-caught mountain trout with her spuds "ox grated," which was as near as Longarm could pronounce the fancy way French folks fixed potatoes.

The senator wanted a T-bone steak smothered with fried onions to go with his plain old mashed spuds and gravy. The Pinkerton man, like Longarm, settled for the roast beef, string bean, and fried potato special of the day. Everyone but Kate went with coffee. She ordered tea, by brand. But of course she'd said she'd been to a finishing school.

As they all ate, taking their time, Longarm got more about the older vet's military career out of the senator. When Kate asked if Longarm had been in the war he shrugged it off. "All of us were young and foolish once,"

17

he said. "I disremember who I rode with or what I might have done. We were talking about the Battle of Glorieta and claims about mistreating prisoners."

The senator sighed. "I rode under Chivington when he was still a major. Say what you may about his later mistakes in that Cheyenne camp along Sand Creek, I never saw him commit any outright atrocities when I was serving under him with the Firsters. It was the *Third* Colorado he was leading when he attacked the wrong Indians at Sand Creek. Johnny Slough was our regimental commander at Glorieta, and he'd have never put up with any dishonorable behavior!"

Trying to word it so as not to upset a lady munching fish, Longarm asked, "Is it true what they say about Chivington and all those Confederate mules near Apache Canyon, sir?"

The senator answered bleakly, "I was there. We butchered the captured supply brutes with sword or bayonet for the same reasons Custer slaughtered those Indian ponies at the Washita. It may sound like cruelty to animals but so might hooking a fish, and you simply don't allow your enemy to go on riding or packing when he moves so much slower afoot!"

Kate Thayer paused, a delicate fork stuck in mountain trout, as she murmured, "Do we have to be so graphic, Senator?"

The older man shrugged. "He asked. I neither boast nor apologize for the little I did in the war as a part-time trooper. I was never promoted to lance corporal as those letters suggest. I did what I was told, to the best of a somewhat younger lawyer's ability. Had Major Chivington ordered me to execute any irregulars, I can't say now what I'd have done. Emotions were running higher back when the world seemed younger and it looked as if Johnny Reb might really grab the Pikes Peak gold fields. I'd like to think I would have said to let George do it. But I *might* have done as I was told. The point is that I never did. We did capture rebel scouts, more than once. At Pigeon Ranch Major Chivington did say something about hanging some, not shooting any, but the matter was settled to the satisfaction of all concerned when those frightened Texans told us everything we'd ever wanted to know about the disposition of their forces. It was the information gleaned from prisoners at Pigeon Ranch that led to our intercepting and wiping out that Confederate supply column near Apache Canyon. We never captured any patrols after that fight. So how could some fool kid from Texas accuse me of having murdered a whole bunch of them with my very own pistol?"

The Pinkerton man suggested, "What if some old reb, trying to whitewash his own betrayal of Confederate secrets, changed his war stories a lot when he told them to his kid?"

Longarm washed down some grub thoughtfully and declared, "I hear heaps of odd war stories from gents who couldn't have much to hide, since they couldn't have done what they say they've done. I find it odd an old self-appointed Johnny Reb would name a particular enemy in Union blue by name, though. It's likely just as well these days that most tales of blood and slaughter fail to include any enemy names and addresses!"

His thoughts drifted off to a peach orchard in bloom at a place called Shiloh as the Pinkerton man asked, "Whatever happened to the infamous Butcher Chivington after he was supposed to have ordered his troops to butcher prisoners, senator?"

Longarm was staring through a priest at the next table, seeing the hurt look in the eyes of an enemy boy about his own age when the world had been young indeed. He was sure glad there'd been no way for that kid to write home the name and address of the West-by-God-Virginia boy who'd come unstuck first and fired just in time.

He managed to return his attention to the table, and sipped some more coffee as the senator finished the sad tale of the Reverend Colonel John Chivington having to resign from both the state militia and the Methodist Church after his bloody errors and foolish speeches at Sand Creek. The Pinkerton man was suggesting the senator lay all the facts before the public, explaining, "Ought to be easy enough to prove no such orders were ever given, or carried out by someone who was never promoted to lance corporal, Senator."

The older man flared. "I can show you my service record if you'd like to accompany me to Guard Headquarters, young sir!"

The Pinkerton man looked confounded. "Hold on. Nobody here said they doubted your word, Senator."

But the distinguished if red-faced politico insisted louder, "I heard that remark about old war stories told by aging windbags, and all right, maybe Glorieta wasn't as big a boo as Gettysburg, but I was there and we did save the Pikes Peak gold field, and all that gold, for Union and Liberty too!"

Kate Thayer said demurely, "So did my father, and he used to talk a lot about winding up in the Battle of Glorieta."

She sipped her tea and added with a puzzled little smile, "He seemed to think it was awfully amusing. I never understood why, once I'd heard how many widows and orphans were left by both sides."

Longarm murmured, "You had to have been in a war to get the joke, ma'am. But before we go offering the senator's old pay book to the *Post* and *Rocky Mountain News* combined, I suggest we commence with a letter writer confused by false facts. Guilty knowledge can give a heap away. Guilty knowledge about things that might have never taken place could give away even more."

He turned to the senator. "You're certain any old militia records still on hand would back your denial that any rebs at all were ever forced to dig their own graves and shot in the napes of their necks by you or anyone else, senator?"

Fraser answered confidently, "I can produce my old records and probably those of every other man who ever rode with the Colorado Volunteers. All three wartime regiments. They are still on file in the governor's archives as well as over at Camp Weld. I can't swear to every action by every unit at a time I was only a middle-aged and very confused recruit. But I can send for all the records on hand if you gents would like to go through them."

Longarm and the Pinkerton man exchanged looks. It was the Pink who said, "I've been meaning to read all the way through the King James Testaments, Old and New, before I pass away. But somehow I never seem to get the time, and surely the complete records of three whole regiments has to read even longer."

The senator suggested, "Maybe there'd be something in the archives of Chivington's Four Hundred! Can't you see the idiot who's been sending Kate and me crazy threats has to have me confounded with some other member of my old battalion?"

Longarm objected. "You just said nobody under Chivington ever murdered any prisoners because Chivington never gave any such fool orders, sir."

The senator looked confused. "I said as far as I *knew*. I was only a part-time soldier dragged into things I never understood at the time. I was still working out hay-foot from straw-foot when the next thing any of us knew we were off to fight the enemy in wild country I'd get lost in today!"

Longarm nodded soberly. "It's likely just as well those Texas boys had about as little training before they found themselves marched off to war. Think how many would have died if any of you had known what he was doing."

The Pinkerton man opined things might have gone the other way in a fight between responsible adults. He got Longarm to agree a grown-up crook could often be reasoned with, while kids and half-wits often chose to go down shooting. Then Durante said, "This unreconstructed

21

rebel writing nasty letters has to be a kid if I add up his own figures right. So he just might mean to carry out his threats. But he admits he wasn't there, and you just heard the senator admit he wasn't watching every move of two widespread outfits from up in a balloon."

The senator asked if there was any point to such speculation. Durante nodded. "Yessir. It's entirely possible a grudge-holding war orphan has you mixed up with somebody else entirely. It could have been a lance corporal from another troop in your battalion, or even someone from a different battalion carrying out the orders of a different officer. Say the letter writer was raised on a garbled version of an inflated war story, inspired by Chivington's later disgrace at Sand Creek. Say some old reb, not knowing who the guilty officer was, just assumed it had to be Butcher Chivington. Say that once he did that, and inspired someone else to lay hands on a roster of Chivington's Four Hundred, well, a Fraser is a Fraser and a lance corporal by any name would smell as unsweet if somebody confused him with a more distinguished veteran of the same battle with a similar name. So say we get our own rosters of all the battalions of the First Colorado Volunteers and—"

"Say the dog had paid attention to the rabbit and just caught the rabbit," Longarm declared. "Your notion makes sense in a time-consuming way, Durante. But no offense, it seems to me we ought to be more worried about the letter writer than who he ought to be writing to. He she or it *thinks* the senator here deserves the blame for Dear Old Dad's demise. We got to accept that as the motive whether those letters are meant seriously or not."

The senator put down his fork, protesting, "I dammit never in my life shot anybody in the nape of the neck! At the risk of spoiling my old war-horse status in the G.A.R., I wouldn't swear on any bible I killed *anybody* during my short military career. There was so much dust and gunsmoke, and the rebs dropped into the chaparral when you shot at them whether they were hit or not!"

Longarm nodded. "I just said that, Senator. At this late date it don't matter. No rational vet of either side would get all that excited about whether a mere lance corporal did or didn't carry out cruel orders more than fifteen years ago. So we're dealing with a crackpot, and have to assume the threats are serious until we can find out where they're coming from."

He saw Kate Thayer had lost interest in her grub, with half of it still on her plate too. So he finished his coffee and declared, "We got to start setting up safer defenses. Do you really have to attend that session this afternoon, Senator?"

Fraser nodded soberly. "I do. The price of silver is of vital interest to a lot of my constituents, including Kathleen here."

Longarm nodded. "*Bueno*. I'd best whip back down to my own office and round up some extra gunhands to guard that gallery right above you all as you fuss about Miss Kate's mines. We hardly need her there with you looking out for her best interests, Senator."

He turned to the girl to tell her, not ask her, "I want you to let Detective Durante take you home from here, ma'am."

She said she'd go if he'd come by later and tell her how he was doing. He said he would and, turning to Durante, asked, "Could you get back from Miss Kate's and cover that gallery till I show up in force, pard?"

Durante nodded. "Sure. But who'll be covering the main target here while I'm on my way to the Thayer place and you're on your way to the Federal Building?"

Longarm said, "He'll be forted up. Since nobody seems to want dessert, I ought to be able to escort the senator back to the State House and leave him behind locked doors till you or I make it back in plenty of time for the afternoon session. Agreed?"

23

Durante said the plan made sense to him. The senator asked for the tab, and told the waitress to keep the change from the fiver he handed her. Like gamblers, politicians tended to be big tippers.

Once they were all outside, the Pinkerton man hailed a passing hansom cab and told Longarm he'd be back to the State House within the hour. So once he'd helped Kate Thayer aboard and they'd seen the two of them off, Longarm and the senator walked back across Colfax to the State House.

Along the way Longarm found out that the older man had told only the senior partners of his law firm about the threats. Despite being a state senator elected from a mining and cattle county over to the west, or because of it, the senator maintained his regular Denver law practice down along Curtis Street, and kept his senatorial staff up on Capitol Hill tending to his purely political chores. When Longarm asked, the senator told him none of his hired help around the State House had been told about the death threats. Nobody he had up that way was a full member of the bar or a partner who'd be affected financially by his being murdered, save for being out of a job.

When Longarm remarked that his sour-faced secretary seemed to be upset enough already, the senator laughed and said, "I think the poor little sparrow is trying to seem older and wiser by sneering at us all like that. I've tried to get her to smile at visitors. That can *really* look unsettling!"

Longarm saw what he meant when they went inside to the senator's office and he was formally introduced to Miss Gordon, as the sour-faced drab was called. She tried to be a sport. Her teeth looked to be sound as she smiled. But she still seemed about to bite his nose off, poor thing.

The senator led the way back to an inner office lined with law books instead of oak paneling. Longarm noted the stout door of soft but thick white pine that was stained mahogany. He felt better when the old trooper from the Colorado Firsters opened a desk drawer to haul out his old Navy Colt from his militia days.

The senator's old .36 had long since been converted to fire brass cartridges, and it was safe to assume an old vet who'd lived through Apache Canyon and Glorieta could hit anybody who made it through a locked door into such a modest chamber. So Longarm warned the senator to sit tight and not open up to anybody until he got back.

When the older man agreed, Longarm went out front and told Miss Gordon to tell anyone who asked that her boss wasn't in.

She didn't ask why. So he decided she couldn't be all bad, despite a distaste for him and the rest of his world.

He ambled out and off across the Capitol grounds, humming that old border ballad about another Miss Gordon he'd learned off some coal-mining folks down the other side of Pueblo. He couldn't have said why, save that both Miss Gordons sounded like stuck-up cunts. The one in the border ballad sounded prettier.

He was striding downhill pretty quickly. So he made it back to the Federal Building in less time than it had taken going the other way. He found Billy Vail fussing with papers, as usual, and he braced for an argument when he explained his need for some support. But Vail was either in a good mood, or impressed by the senator's stand on silver. Either way, he said he'd send Smiley and Dutch on up to the State House if they ever got back from their free lunch and expensive draft at the Parthenon.

That freed Longarm to retrace his steps. They were commencing to add up when he mounted the State House steps a third time that same day. But a deputy marshal was more used to working on his feet than your average rider.

He caught the sour-faced Miss Gordon filing her nails. So she did care what others thought of her after all. He asked her if she'd ever heard the sad song about Miss

25

Peggy Gordon. She said she had and told him not to be silly. So he went on back to see the senator some more.

The older man was pleased to see him back so soon. He said he'd been worried about showing up late for that afternoon session down the hall. Longarm said, "I figure you still have better than twenty minutes if they meant what they said about starting some more around one o'clock, sir. Why don't you let me go on up to the gallery and have a look-see before you mosey back to that senate chamber?"

The senator agreed to sit tight a full fifteen minutes by his own watch. That sounded good enough for Longarm. He figured he could make it upstairs and win or lose a gunfight in fifteen minutes.

It took him less than five to climb the marble steps and stride the impressively gloomy hallway to the open doorway of the public gallery. As he glided through it he saw some old jaspers were already drifting in down below, and the chairman of the senate was sharing a state secret or a dirty joke with some other old jaspers. Nobody was up in the gallery save for himself and Detective Durante, in a seat down at the far end.

The Pinkerton man didn't seem to have noticed Longarm's silent entrance. Longarm called quietly out to the inattentive cuss as he worked his way there along the back of the seats.

When the Pink paid no attention Longarm swore and raised his voice. "Have you been drinking in the few minutes I ain't been watching you, sleepyhead?"

The Pink didn't answer. He just sat there with his chin on his chest, as if he'd fallen asleep sitting up. Longarm swore and said, "I'm sure glad I got back before the session started down yonder, you less-than-useless cuss!"

Then he looked closer, bent forward to grip Durante's shoulder as it suddenly got ten degrees colder up there in the gloom, and murmured, "Sorry, pard. I thought you'd fallen asleep on the job."

26

It took him a few moments later to determine what had killed the detective. There were no visible wounds until Longarm forked a leg over the seats and moved the Pink's still-warm body forward off the seat back he'd been leaned against.

Durante had been stabbed in the back, probably as he'd stepped through that doorway. Then his killer or killers had hauled him to a seat as far from the doorway as possible so that . . . what?

Longarm whirled, .44-40 in hand, to stare at nothing but that open doorway to the empty hall, feeling mighty confounded but not the least bit foolish. For it took someone good to take out a Pink on the prod. And worse yet, the killer or killers were still on the prowl most anywhere you wanted to guess at!

Chapter 3

Longarm found a couple of elderly Capitol guards guarding their coffeepot and checkerboard in the basement. From the way the two of them moved, and the way they carried on once they got to the public gallery, he suspected neither had seen more recent action than the two brass cannons out front. But at least they secured the gallery and kept the public out till Smiley and Dutch showed up from the Federal Building with their Winchesters.

Deputy Smiley hadn't smiled in human memory. Smiley was his name. He was a tall morose breed, part Pawnee or maybe Osage. It didn't matter. He'd fought Lakota, Comanche, and other hostiles in his day, and could be just as firm but fair with white troublemakers.

The deputy called Dutch, because nobody could pronounce his German name, was a short stocky cuss who always had a ready smile and a wry joke for everybody, whether he was fixing to kill them or not. The boss, Marshal Vail, liked to team the two of them because the gloomy Smiley could usually keep the grinning Dutch out of totally uncalled-for gunfights. Smiley, Marshal Vail, and naturally Longarm were the only gents in the outfit who could tell Dutch he was acting like an asshole and live.

The argument about silver down on the senate floor had gone on for some time when Smiley and Dutch showed up. Longarm had felt no need to roll the dead Pink over the balcony rail, and the senators on the floor below were used to odd commotions in the public gallery. Hence they paid them no mind.

Longarm had already placed the dead detective on his back with his hands across his chest out of consideration for Durante's kith and kin. The blankly staring face was already sort of pale and waxen. Nobody but the coroner and his forensic crew, along with the undertaker of the family's choice, would ever notice the liver-to-purple discoloration of the lower regions of the cadaver as its blood cells settled out of the straw-colored serum of uncirculating gore.

One of the old guards was listening with interest as Longarm brought his fellow federal men up to date on the death threats. It was just as well he had been when Smiley, the born pessimist, said, "Oh, I don't know. Cranks who write letters well in advance hardly ever turn up to menace anyone face-to-face. I've met up with that Pink on the floor. He was good. I don't see how anyone he didn't know could have gotten close enough to stab him, even in the back. You say Durante was up here keeping an eye on the back of that senator who says he fought at Glorieta? I've met heaps of vets who fought at Glorieta. I doubt some were ever in any outfit, judging by other dumb things they say. Have you talked to anyone who served with the senator in the Colorado Firsters, Longarm?"

The old Capitol guard cut in to say, "He has. He's talked to *me*. I rid with the Colorado First Volunteers, but not with the Bloody Third. There may have been a few old boys from the First and Second Regiments at Sand Creek, but it was Chivington's Third Colorado as we have to thank for history writers saying all the Colorado Volunteers did in the war was slaughter Indians."

Smiley muttered, "I had to ask, and there went a grand notion."

Longarm said, "It wasn't all that grand as soon as you consider it was the senator who asked for our help. Say he never served at all, or say every word of those accusing letters could be true. The man would have no sensible reason to call on us for anything. Gents out to cover guilty secrets only have to keep their traps shut. I'm sure the old gent is sincerely worried about those death threats, and now that I gaze down on poor Durante there, I'm starting to worry too!"

Dutch put a thoughtful hand on the balcony rail and leaned out a tad before he hauled his Stetson back in out of the light and wondered, "Why would even a crackpot out to take revenge on anyone back-stab a poor cuss guarding the intended victim's back and then just leave?"

Smiley started to tell him he was an asshole. But then the breed scowled down at all those bobbing heads and nodded. "When you're right you're right, Dutch. If Durante was on guard alone up here, no matter who did what to him, or how, the killer would have wound up all alone up here with a clear shot at most anyone on the senate floor! He had the time, and opportunity, to kill the real object of his stored-up bile, even with a well-aimed flowerpot!"

Longarm suggested, "Maybe he didn't have a flowerpot. Or maybe he wants the senator, and us, to sweat some more, now that we've had a convincing demonstration of his lethal intentions!"

Smiley decided, "Well, you did say this dead Pink here thought you were dealing with some kind of lunatic. It does seem as if a war orphan out to kill a father's executioner would just up and kill him, unless he wanted him to anticipate a mite. The senator figures to shit or go blind when he finds out about about this. Mayhaps the killer feels that's worth the disadvantage his letter writing has him at with *us*."

The old guard asked what disadvantage Smiley was talking about, since it hadn't prevented the death of a lawman on the prod for his killer.

Dutch chuckled and observed, "You'd best hang a wreath on your nose to let the neighbors know your brain is dead, Pop. What would the four of us be jawing about right now if the asshole hadn't sent them threatening letters? None of us federal men would even be here, and you'd be telling some copper badge from Denver P.D. how some visitor found the cuss dead and you had no ideas at all about who killed him."

The guard said, "But wouldn't Senator Fraser . . ." Then he nodded sheepishly. "Right. He wouldn't know anyone was after him if the killer hadn't sent all those death threats!"

"So Durante would still be alive," said Longarm. "Because nobody would have hired him in the first place. It's like what the world would be like today if that murder plot against Caesar had failed, or even one of those attempts to murder Good Queen Bess had succeeded. Remind me to get somebody to explain that silver bill they're fussing about down yonder. Now that I think back, I tried to get the senator not to attend that very session and . . . Shit, why *didn't* they throw that flowerpot Smiley suggested?"

Smiley said, "Maybe they never heard me. Do you want one of us to go find a copper badge to fetch us a meat wagon, Longarm?"

The tall deputy in charge started to object. Then he shrugged. "Yep, it is the county coroner's case once you study on it. We're going to have a hell of a chore keeping half of this shit out of the newspapers, boys."

The Capitol guard asked why they wanted to. He'd likely never had his name in the *Rocky Mountain News* before. Dutch chuckled in an easygoing way and said, "Because it's a *federal* case, you dumb shit."

31

Longarm intervened. "Now children, don't fight. I'm sure there'll be enough for everybody. The story has to come out sooner or later, and the sooner Denver P.D. gets on it the less pissed off they'll act."

The old Capitol guard volunteered to go find some local law. So Longarm let him, waiting until he'd left before he muttered, "Billy Vail and the Justice Department would doubtless just as soon saddle Denver with all the round-the-clock policing this is adding up to."

So Dutch said, "I follow your drift. So fuck 'em. Let them have some of the chores if they can't stay out of our beeswax!"

Longarm had finished jotting down everything he could think of by the time that one guard returned with two Denver roundsmen and the redoubtable Sergeant Nolan of the D.P.D. Fortunately, Longarm was on good terms with Nolan, who like Dutch could shoot first and wonder why later. Longarm put his notebook away, and had started to fill the copper badges in when Nolan barked at one of his men to fetch a meat wagon from the downtown morgue.

Nolan naturally knew Senator Fraser and where he stayed most of the time in the state capital. "It's a grand brownstone he holds in his sister's name over on Logan Street, not far from that Tabor mansion where you and me broke up that burglary ring that time."

Longarm nodded, picturing a Capitol Hill address about two long and two short blocks from the south side of the State House. He felt no call to ask dumb questions about the legal residence of a senator elected from a mining district on the far side of the Platte. Nobody with a lick of sense expected Colorado statesmen to be anywhere but Denver when they weren't up in the hills buying drinks or kissing babies. He mentioned a police guard to Nolan. The sergeant said he didn't care, since he'd not be standing there in the dark in the wee small hours, but that Longarm, or better yet Billy Vail, would have to clear it with his precinct captain.

The Capitol guard at the door almost stopped the next visitor before he recognized Senator Fraser and let him through. The silver-haired older man asked, "Have I been missing something down on the floor, Deputy Long? When I noticed all these uniforms up here I . . . Jesus H. Christ, what's Detective Durante doing there on the floor?"

Longarm told him dryly, "We were just talking about that. He was sitting up when I first found him. Either way, he'd been stabbed in the back."

The senator gasped. "My God! Is he dead?"

It was Dutch who cheerfully volunteered, "Dead as a turd in a milk bucket. Did you do it, Senator? We were just saying he likely knew his killer well enough to trust him."

The senator's jaw dropped and he protested, "See here, I was in my office, with a secretary between me and the hall, until I went directly down the first-story hall and out onto the floor, where I've been until just now!"

Longarm said, "Shut up, Dutch. You're talking dumber than you usually do, and it was my suggestion the senator here do just like he told you. Durante ate his noon dinner with the senator and me—alive, of course. Then he carried the senator's ward, Miss Kate Thayer, to her home in the same condition. *She* couldn't have stabbed Durante either, because he came back to the State House alive, to get killed up here whilst the senator and me were together down in his office. He was still in his office as I left it to come directly upstairs and find this poor Pink dead. I just laid out all them dumb details because I thought it might be helpful to Sergeant Nolan here, or because I'm starting to get sick of assholes grasping at straws. We got enough on our plates without speculating on every remotely possible suspicion. It's *possible* George Washington was a British spy. Just as it's *possible* there used to be a land called Atlantis out in the middle of the main ocean. But let's stick to the damned old rules of evidence and go with what we know. We know the senator here had a mess of death threats sent to him. We know his ward, Miss Kate Thayer, got a nasty letter accusing the senator of war crimes. We know the senator called on the federal government for help whilst the gal hired herself a private detective."

He turned to the senator. "Did you know Miss Kate had been in touch with the Pinks before she told you in front of me, sir?"

When the older man blinked and asked how he could have known, Longarm said, "Good question. And you couldn't have killed him even if you had known, since what reason would you have to murder a man hired to guard you?"

He hesitated, then bit the bullet, and asked, "Where would it leave Kate Thayer if you were to suddenly bite the dust, Senator?"

The old trustee of the Thayer estate shrugged. "It would have no effect on her finances, if that's what you mean."

Longarm said, "That's what I meant. She's already told me about a junior partner simply taking over. I feel even better hearing it from you. But whilst we're on the subject, and seeing they're still jawing about it down on the floor, what difference would it make to the price of silver if somebody laid you low before the matter could be decided one way or the other, sir?"

The elder stateman smiled wistfully. "One senate vote. My side's motion would still carry. We have the majority required to stay with President Hayes and his sound-money policy. That populist tripe about free silver is more hot air than fire, despite or perhaps because of all the passionate orations we've been sitting through all week. I don't see any reason for the free-silver utopians to single me out in particular. I'm only one man, and nobody but boobs and idiots considers free silver the cure for the common cold."

Then he cocked his head and listened. "They're about to vote on a rider to the stupid bill and I'm going to have

34

to get back down to the floor, gentlemen."

Nobody saw fit to stop him. As he was leaving, Longarm asked if he'd be at home to callers that evening. The senator shot back he had a supper engagement, but that he'd likely be home by nine. After he left, Sergeant Nolan said that gave them plenty of time to set up a police guard with the house servants.

A few minutes later a wary morgue attendant came up to ask if there was really somebody dead up there. As Nolan led him over to the cadaver sort of wedged between the front seats and the balcony railing, Longarm asked Deputy Smiley, "Could you tag along and take care of the paperwork Billy Vail's sure to want old Henry to file? I got some tedious legwork of my own this afternoon."

The saturnine breed said, "Sure. I know how to write. Where're you headed, over to Guard Headquarters to paw through old records of the Colorado Firsters?"

Longarm shook his head. "Not hardly. Taking the letter writer at face value for now, Confederate war orphans would hardly be listed on the rosters of the Colorado Volunteers."

Smiley suggested, "Dear Old Dad might, as a captured rebel."

Longarm smiled thinly and replied, "I've yet to read official records of atrocities committed by the side doing the recording. The senator says he neither witnessed nor heard tell of such goings-on as described in that letter to Kate Thayer. I've no call to disbelieve him. So it's likely safe to say that if it happened at all, it happened somewhere else on a spread-out field of battle and never got bragged about. An officer who misbehaves in the heat of battle and decides to cover up after he's cooled down would hardly file a written report for his own side's archives."

"So where do you figure to look at this late date?" asked Smiley.

Longarm replied, "The only place there might be some written record. In the Confederate archives, of course."

Chapter 4

The main branch of the Denver Public Library stood just down the other side of Broadway with other municipal buildings facing the State Capitol grounds. Longarm spent a lot of time there near the end of each month, when reading was the only secret vice he could afford. But there was forbidden lore the Denver Public Library didn't stock, and not all of it was pornographic.

The gold placers of nearby Cherry Creek had been discovered by the Ralston brothers, members of the civilized Cherokee Nation who'd adopted more civilized names. They'd bottomed out their modest claim on a tributary of Cherry Creek and moved on to nobody cared where. But their run of luck had been noted by far more serious gold seekers from the older Eastern gold fields of Georgia.

Most folks had forgotten by now how the first gold rush north of Old Mexico had occurred, way back before the famous California Rush, in the piney hills of Northwest Georgia. But it had, and so the first Yankee gold miners, although they'd now feel insulted by the term, had been from the Old South.

Thus the Colorado Gold Rush of '59 had been spearheaded by the Russel brothers out of Georgia, in tough competition with John Easter from Bleeding Kansas and his considerable train of wagons marked "Pikes Peak or Bust."

Many went bust, while others, of all races and political stripes, got rich or killed by Arapaho, who suffered under the delusion that Manitou had created their hunting grounds for *them*.

The Indian menace and the interest in gold kept the rough tough early settlers more or less at peace until Fort Sumter. Four days later somebody hoisted the Bonnie Blue Flag of the Confederacy over Wallington & Murphy's Store on Sixteenth Street and the fun began.

The Unionists won. Vigilantes called The Stranglers drove the pro-"Secesh" out, or inspired them to just lie low and wait for the redemption of Colorado Territory by Sibley's Texas Brigade.

That had never happened, thanks to the Battle of Glorieta. But a man could dream, both before and after. So a rich old mining magnate called Stratton had amassed one hell of a library of Confederate lore before he'd passed away. Hence Longarm had found the old gold miner's private reading a gold mine of helpful hints about unreconstructed rebels who still liked to stop trains and rob banks.

Longarm had befriended the Strattons, catching highgraders for them, before old Warren Stratton had died of an ague. His widow, the ancient but still fluttery Miss Magnolia, had gone on letting Longarm borrow books from her late husband's big collection. He always brought them back, and the fluttery old lady seemed to enjoy his company.

So Longarm was braced for some fluttery fan-waving and at least one cup of weak tea as he stood at the door of the Stratton place on Penn Street around three o'clock. An elderly colored man the Widow Stratton called "Uncle," despite being just as old as she was, usually came to the door. So Longarm was surprised, two ways, when a younger white lady, maybe ten years older than he was, opened the door in a scarlet silk robe.

It wouldn't have been polite to suggest it might have been more proper to close the robe all the way before opening a front door. But nothing serious showed, and what did wasn't displeasing to gaze upon.

He told the brunette with her hair let down who he was and what he'd come for. He said he'd try somewhere else when she allowed that her Dear Cousin Magnolia was visiting other kin. But she said to come right in and that he could call her Lee, since everybody did, even though her full name was Lidia.

She didn't say anything about tea. As she led the way back to the library, down a long hallway that looked as if it belonged in some old church, she explained she'd just taken a bath and had yet to decide how she might want to dress for the coming evening. She said she hardly knew anyone out here in Denver. So he had to ask where she hailed from, and wasn't surprised to learn she came from Alabama without a banjo to her name. It was her joke. Longarm wondered why it made her giggle so.

The library he doubtless knew better than she did was well lit by a bay window overlooking the well-kept backyard. Well kept until recently, leastways. When the dandelions sprouting on the patch of back lawn inspired Longarm to casually ask about the usual butler, Lee said Uncle Plato had gone East along east with his mistress, Miss Magnolia, and added, "That means we have the whole place to our very own. Are you frightened, Custis?"

He blinked in confusion and asked if she thought the house was haunted.

She batted her lashes and sort of purred, "Oh, come now, Cousin Magnolia has told me all about you. You are the same Custis Long they call Long One, aren't you?"

He chuckled and allowed that was close enough as he moved over to the bookcase. He was sort of confused by all those titles to pick from too.

The oddly behaved brunette waited as if expecting him to say or do something odd, shrugged when he didn't, and said something about fetching them some refreshments.

He wanted to tell her not to. But it wasn't his house. Had it been a real library there'd have been a sign warning folks to shut up and let others study. But if old Magnolia had told Lee about his earlier visits, she'd have likely explained how he liked to go through the books without her after a few minutes of polite conversation with tea and crumpets. He wondered how mention of his fairly rare visits could have left any impression at all on a younger lady visiting from the Southeast. There were surely more interesting things in Colorado to jaw about than a lawman who came by to look something up now and again.

He found what seemed a privately printed war memoir by an old reb describing himself as a Captain C.S.A. commanding a howitzer battery of Sibley's Texas Brigade. From conversations at the Parthenon Longarm knew Chivington's Battalion of the Colorado Firsters had cut off a heap of mountain artillery at Apache Canyon, and the artillery had sent scouts, or spies, out ahead to spot likely targets.

He set that book aside for future reading on a stand by the big old cushioned sofa across the bay window. He found another memoir he'd already read sometime back. He knew it was sort of self-serving and blamed Sibley's retreat on those "Union Regulars" from Fort Union. He hadn't been digging for war crimes the last time he'd leafed through it, but it was the sort of crybaby war chronicle you'd expect to see crimes mentioned in, if there was any justification at all. So he put that with the other.

Before he could find a third book, the gal who liked to be called Lee came back in pushing a whole tea wagon. But the cut-glass ewer on the silver tea tray was filled with ice and what looked like red wine. She said it was a real French burgundy meant to go with the fancy biscuits, runny cheese, and something she called patted fat grass. He'd never heard of icing red table wine. But he didn't argue as she sat him on the sofa, sank down beside him, and poured them both healthy drinks in brandy snifters. He wasn't braced for the sloe gin she'd laced the wine with, and almost gave himself away as a sissy by gasping while she buttered him some biscuits with soft cheese and that patted fat grass.

The laced wine tasted better washing down grub. The runny cheese was better than it smelled, and the patted fat grass turned out to be just a fancy name for chopped goose liver. When he asked why she was going so light on it herself, Lee said she'd already eaten. After he confessed he'd had his own dinner well after high noon, she told him not to eat too much if he wasn't hungry. Then she leaned back, letting her robe open in a downright saucy way, as she demurely asked if there were any other manly appetites she could satisfy for such a distinguished visitor.

Longarm wasn't as country as he talked. So he figured calling a deputy marshal distinguished was meant to be sardonic. He didn't get sore. He suspected that, like her giggling at odd times, Lee's veiled hints likely covered some awkwardness she felt for some reason. But he wasn't there to determine why a no-longer-young brunette from Alabama might feel awkward amid strange surroundings. He was out to determine who might be sending death threats to a state senator. So he started to explain why he wanted to borrow those three books.

Lee didn't seem interested in his job with the Justice Department. Yawning on purpose, she asked, "Would it save us any time if I assured you Cousin Magnolia has told me *all* about you, Custis?"

Then she looked away, blushing becomingly all the way down the V of her partly open robe, as he wondered what in thunder old Widow Stratton could have told her.

He knew there was some gossip up here on Capitol Hill about him and another widow woman over on Sherman, south of the State House. It made a man feel odd to think they were gossiping over fences this far to the northeast. For it wasn't as if he and that far younger widow had been doing it dog-style on the front lawn in broad day, and she was really going to be upset if she heard doing it in the dark behind closed curtains hadn't worked.

Not knowing what to say, he washed down some more patted fat grass with her fancy firewater. She murmured, "Good idea. Maybe we should get tipsy first. I'm not usually this shy, but frankly you're a little frightening in the flesh. It was one thing to hear Magnolia simply describe you as a muscular Adonis hung like a horse. But now that I've seen how big and, well, sure of yourself you seem up close . . ."

Longarm laughed incredulously. "I'm sure of myself? I don't even know what we're talking about, ma'am?"

She smiled up at him radiantly. "You're not one to kiss and tell, eh? I like that in a man. It's so hard for a warm-natured grass widow to meet really sophisticated men with any prowess in bed. It seems an adventurous woman has to choose between a stud who brags about it later in the barbershop and a sensitive well-mannered type who simply isn't worth going to bed with!"

Longarm gulped, but forced his eyes to meet her flashing brown ones as he quietly asked, "Has somebody told you I've been going to bed with Miss Magnolia, Miss Lee?"

She was the one who first looked away, cheeks aglow, and she told him, "Mostly on this very sofa, to hear her tell it. I confess I had to laugh the first time she confessed her secret passion for a man young enough to be her son. But on reflection I saw what wise Ben Franklin had in mind when he advised younger men to leave the young virgins alone and take up with older women."

Longarm had to laugh. Like everyone else, he'd read the possibly forged but amusing letter Franklin was supposed

41

to have written to a younger kinsman starting out in a new town.

Longarm found himself reciting. "Like trees, women first begin to wither at the top, retaining their form and juices further down for a prudent woodsman to cut into."

The older brunette untied her sash and let her red robe fall away from firm breasts, flat belly, and hirsute mound of Venus as she continued reciting. "They're more experienced, more discreet, and above all, more *grateful* than any silly young maid one can hope to meet!"

So Longarm got rid of his hat, shoved the tea wagon out of the way with a boot heel, and hauled her in for some howdy-do. For it felt awkward undressing in broad daylight with a gal before you'd at least swapped some spit and felt her up a mite.

By the time he had, Lee was out of her robe entirely and trying to unbutton him all at once as she pleaded, with her moist lips against his, "Hurry! Oh, my God, hurry!"

So he did, telling her it was all right if she only called him by his mortal name, seeing they'd become too informal.

She laughed like hell, then stiffened in wonder as he rolled into the welcoming saddle of her wide-spread thighs to enter her at last. It felt swell to him too as he found her as tight and juicy as old Ben Franklin had suggested he might. She moved her hips to meet his thrusts. But then, she'd allowed she might be experienced. He thrust harder and faster. It was the least he could do for another older woman who'd been kind to him. He knew he was doing the gallant thing when this one sobbed, "Ooh, Magnolia was right! There ought to be a law against such wonderfully hot screwing!"

He didn't tell the out-of-state gal that, as a matter of fact, there was. Colorado had severe statutes prohibiting fornication between man and sheep, goats, burros, or other critters as well as ladies they weren't married to. But since such fornicating ladies as Madame Ruth Jacobs, Emma

42

Gould, or Squirrel Tooth Alice had not been arrested recently, a discreet grass widow from Alabama was likely safe to screw, and he really needed those three books.

The horny grass widow, after admitting she hadn't had a full dozen lovers since her divorce, made Longarm earn the right to read the books as the afternoon wore on toward evening. She came with him in the old-fashioned way, then came with him dog-style, and on top when he just had to stop and have a smoke.

Squatting atop him, still throbbing around his semi-erection, Lee suddenly blurted out nervously, "We don't want Cousin Magnolia to know about this, do we? I mean, she boasted about you pleasuring her this way, even allowing for exaggeration. But when she told me to just make myself at home, I don't think she meant for me to go this far, do you?"

He took a luxurious drag on his smoke and said soothingly, "You just told me you admired men who could be discreet. I swear I'll never tell Miss Magnolia about all this."

Chapter 5

Sweating in a sunny bay window with a juicy older woman could inspire a man to feel pungent. But Lee said she'd draw him a bath upstairs if he'd let her get in the tub with him. So he did, and that was fun too. But it was after quitting time when he finally made it back to the Federal Building.

Smiley and Dutch had come and gone. But old Henry never left ahead of the boss, and Marshal Vail was still in the back. Longarm felt no call to disturb him, especially when Henry handed him a carbon of the autopsy report on that dead Pink.

There were no surprises. Longarm had already noticed Durante had been stabbed in the back. The report said the blade had been long and narrow, like a bayonet or stiletto. The killer had slipped it in between the shoulder blade and spine to cut Durante's heart half clear of its moorings. He'd bled to death inside with his aorta sliced clean in two.

Longarm carried those three books to a sit-down bean-ery he knew, and skimmed through them in a booth as he enjoyed an easygoing supper consisting of no more than a steak smothered in chili con pollo, apple pie with cheddar cheese, and three cups of coffee. All that patted fat grass had sort of spoiled his appetite.

Like most self-educated readers, Longarm had learned to skip lots of tedious wordage meant to pad what a man needed to know into a long self-important tome. So he paid no mind to the events leading up to or coming after the fighting around Glorieta Pass back in '62. Two versions made no mention at all of prisoners being executed by either side. But the self-serving whine about the Texicans almost winning did mention a lost patrol. It never said a state senator or anybody else had murdered them in cold blood. But Longarm got out his notebook and took down the names anyway, once he read how a mounted five-man diamond from Pyron's Battalion had vanished into limbo, scouting between Apache Canyon and Pigeon Ranch, about where Butcher Chivington's Four Hundred had been tear-assing in circles through the chaparral.

A Corporal Lew Alcott had led Troopers Bascom, McArtle, Masters, and Wallace into something they'd never gotten out of. The West Texas vet who'd written about them said they'd never come back from the war, and that repeated requests to the Yankees for word of their final fates had been in vain. Their names had never appeared on any roll of prisoners in any Union camp. They'd just ridden off into the heat and dust and never been seen or heard of again. Things like that still happened in Indian country or along the border. Civilians back home were inclined to suspect somebody was covering something up, since it was tough to picture how spread out the country west of, say, Longitude 100 could look to somebody riding across it.

Finding nothing more interesting than that one slim lead, the well-fed but unsatisfied Longarm left the books for safekeeping with a night watchman at the nearby Federal Building and, getting tired of all this infernal walking, treated himself to the hire of a livery mount from that place near the stagecoach depot on Tremont.

The senator had said he'd be dining out till nine, and Longarm had told Kate Thayer he'd be by her place as well. So he rode up Nineteenth to the imposing baby castle the spinster's father had left her.

Kate Thayer's butler, a middle-aged white cuss who looked as if he could smell horseshit clean from the bay tethered to the hitching post out front, told Longarm he was expected and led him on back to yet another library, or study, where the much younger and full-dressed heiress was seated by another bay window, albeit on a Louis XV chair with gilt bow legs. She rose to wave him to a matching seat by the window, and had her help trained so well she never had to tell the snooty butler he'd better get some coffee and cake in there.

Seated with his hat on his knees, since he hadn't let the snooty butler take it away from him, Longarm found she'd already heard about Durante and thought it was just horrid. He felt no call to mention severed aortas. He was telling her about that lost patrol, consulting his own notes for the names, when another servant, this one a pretty little gal in black and white maid's livery, wheeled a whole lot of coffee, tea, and pastry in. It was a caution how Kate Thayer kept her shape so firm while living this soft. But he'd noticed rich gals usually looked at least ten years younger than poor gals the same age.

The French-looking maid had a nice ass too. He wondered why he was noticing such things already after the afternoon he'd had. Maybe Ben Franklin had left out the part about silly young things looking even more tempting after a gent had been kissing a sort of distinguished-looking older face.

Kate Thayer brought him back to common sense as he realized she'd just asked a sensible question. He nodded and said, "You can see the sad tale of that lost rebel patrol don't prove much. I can see dozens of ways to lose a patrol. But who's to say what a worried family down Texas way could have been told about even one of those missing Texas boys?"

He tore his wistful eyes from the interesting rear view of that maid as she was leaving and continued. "It's a long shot. But at least it's a shot, Miss Kate. The book I just mentioned only gives the names. Texas ought to have a muster of Sibley's Brigade on file somewhere, and now that President Hayes has ended the Reconstruction, old rebels are coming out of the woodwork to crow about eating cucumbers and all their other wonders."

She gestured at the pots on the tea table, and when he pointed out the coffee she began to pour some for both of them as she asked in an intelligent tone, "Could the surviving kin of all five missing men possibly blame one Colorado senator for their deaths in wartime?"

He reached for his cup and one of those fancy petty floors as he replied. "No saying what any of 'em might have been told by one or more returning guerrillas with a vivid imagination, ma'am. But I only have to worry about the married-up riders who left widows and orphans behind. And after that, I might be able to narrow her down even further."

He found the French pastry a mite cloying, and washed it down with unsugared coffee before asking if she still had that letter about her family lawyer, the state senator.

She said, "Of course. But didn't I already give you a copy?"

He nodded. "Yep. Typewritten. Why don't you keep the copy and let me have the original in case I find me some handwriting to match up with it?"

He'd already noticed she seemed bright. She nodded soberly and sprang up to move over to a fold-up secretary desk across the study. She opened the writing flap and got an envelope from a pigeonhole as he tried another petty floor and found he'd guessed right about its bittersweet chocolate icing.

As she returned to hand him the postmarked envelope addressed to her she said, "Surely you don't suspect I'd be getting something like this in one handwriting while

47

all those death threats to the senator were in another?"

He only glanced at the envelope, noting the Santa Fe postmark and the clear but sort of schoolkid handwriting before he put it in an inside breast pocket. "I don't know what I ought to suspect yet, Miss Kate. Before Detective Durante wound up dead, I was inclined to buy his notion we were dealing with some harmless crank. Folks write threatening letters as a rule because they're sore about something and don't have the gumption for a face-to-face showdown."

He sipped more coffee and thoughtfully added, "Of course, Durante wasn't allowed a face-to-face showdown, and a sneak who'd stab a man in the back might write unsigned sneaky letters as well. The motive might be to let the intended victim know in advance he's an intended victim. I can see how someone nursing a grudge for years and planning dozens of dark revenges might not care to simply drygulch a man who'd never know he was in trouble before his troubles were over forever."

He tried a bitty cube of pastry that looked as if it might be iced with butterscotch. It was walnut, but what the hell. So he sipped at his cup thoughtfully and admitted, "If the truth be known, I don't know hardly anything. I've barely started scouting for sign, and did you ever read that tale by Mr. Poe about the purloined letter?"

She brightened. "You mean the one where the detectives are searching the quarters of a known spy for a secret letter they know he's stolen, only they can't find it because he's hidden it in plain sight among the papers atop his writing table?"

Longarm nodded. "I sure like that cautionary tale. I've found lots of things the last place a lawman would think to look, in plain sight. I'm trying to keep my mind cleared of logical motives or mental pictures of probable suspects till I read some real sign that really leads somewhere."

Somewhere in the house a clock was chiming. Longarm decided not to go for that petty floor with the green icing after all, and told his pretty hostess he still had to get on over to the Fraser place before it got too late for polite calling.

She saw him to the door instead of leaving it to her snooty old butler or pretty young maid. He knew she had to be pushing thirty, from either direction, but she sure looked young and pretty there in the soft light as he fought back the temptation to kiss her good night as if he'd bought those petty floors for her himself at some fancy place. They shook hands and parted more like pals instead.

He went out to the livery pony waiting at the cast-iron hitching post and untethered it, saying, "I know you'd like to get back to your stall and a bedtime snack of rolled oats, old gal. But we got one more call to make before I give you the lead and let you trot us back to your stable."

The steady mare he'd chosen didn't argue as he swung up aboard her stock saddle and headed south along the tree-lined and deserted street. There were stone-fronted houses on either side, accounting for what might have passed for an echo if the clopping hooves of two mounts had been keeping better time.

Longarm reined to a slower walk. It took the other hoof clops a few moments to change pace as well. Longarm heeled his mount faster. So did somebody else, too far back to make out in the poor lighting of a residential street at this hour. He rode on as if satisfied he had the street to himself. For all he knew he did. There was no law saying another rider couldn't be using a public right-of-way through a residential neighborhood during regular calling hours. The other rider might simply be trying to avoid meeting up with anyone he or she might not know on a dark street. Who said only a lawman out scouting for sign was the only one allowed to spook?

He rode on a few furlongs and, damn it, that rider behind him *was* keeping pace, gauging the distance between them by the sounds of Longarm's old livery mare. The livery breed was tall for a cow pony, but shorter of leg than a thoroughbred. So Longarm could tell the cuss tailing him was riding a high-stepper he had to keep reining in lest he get too close.

Longarm warned himself, "Hold on. Don't draw too tight a picture. For all you know for certain, it could be a gal riding sidesaddle!"

That hardly seemed likely when, figuring he was well south of the Capitol grounds that broke up the street grid of Capitol Hill, Longarm turned a corner and heeled his livery pony to a trot. For the high-stepper out of sight but just within earshot started to trot at the same pace.

By the time it was turning that same corner, Longarm had swung up the alley running between Logan and Sherman. His pony seemed a mite confused. But Longarm said, "I know what I'm doing," as he turned in by a carriage house opening into the alley and reined her to a sudden halt.

Back near the alley mouth his unknown admirer seemed to be doing the same. Longarm took his feet out of the stirrups as he tied the reins to the horn of his hired stock saddle. Then he hauled his feet up, braced his boot heels where his ass usually went, and leaped up off his startled mount to grab the rain gutter of the carriage house, a good thirteen feet above the alley's cinder paving.

His hired pony naturally spooked and ran for home as Longarm did a pull-over to put himself on the sloped roof of the carriage house with a clump the other rider never heard. For the other rider sensed he'd been the victim of another ruse entirely, and tore after what sounded like Longarm's sudden bolt. So he was sitting tall in the saddle like a big-ass bird when Longarm landed on him like a cougar jumping a passing deer from a tree limb.

They landed together on the alley cinders, with Longarm on top. He pistol-whipped the bastard good in case the fall hadn't done it. But when he sat up on the mystery rider's chest to amiably ask him who the fuck he was, he saw that something had done it. His victim was out like a light— one could only hope.

Still holding his .44–40, Longarm thumbnailed a match head afire for a view of what he'd just wrought. In the flickering light of the wax Mex match he saw he'd downed a well-dressed actor, pimp, or whatever. He fired three shots at the sky and put the match to some alley trash he could reach without getting off the pretty boy's chest. So they had more light on the subject when the cuss he'd pinned opened his glassy eyes and muttered, through his split lip, "Where am I? What are you doing on top of me? Don't you know who I am, you lout?"

Longarm said, "Nope. I was just fixing to ask and you'd better not lie. I just called the law with this pissoliver and the neighborhood copper badges will know if you belong around here or not."

His victim groaned, "I don't *belong* around here. I *own* around here. I'm Jefferson Pryce the Third, and I was about to pay my respects to Miss Kate Thayer when I saw a total stranger slipping away from her door and decided to follow him!"

"Don't ever do that again, even if you're telling the truth," said Longarm not unkindly.

Pryce said he was ready to get up. Longarm said he wasn't ready to let him. To his credit the pretty boy knew better than to struggle with a man who had twenty pounds and a gun on him.

So a few minutes later a couple of neighborhood rounds-men they both knew showed up to confirm that Longarm had indeed been sitting on a pillar of Denver Society. By this time they'd both had time to explain a few things to one another, and old Jeff seemed to take it like a sport when Longarm said he was sorry and helped him back to his feet.

The society gent said he didn't want to call on any lady afoot with a split lip and the seat of his pants split. So Longarm asked the copper badges if they'd see him home and make sure his horse had made it as well.

Old Jeff shook on it with him, and allowed that he was glad they were on the same side after all. Longarm was too polite to allow that he took that with a grain of salt. A green-eyed swain who'd track an innocent caller like a Cheyenne Crooked Lancer out for hair seemed as capable as anyone else of writing silly letters.

But they all parted friendly and, knowing his hired mount was well on her way home by now, Longarm legged it on down to the nearby town house the senator kept in his sister's name.

It was the sister Longarm found home alone, save for the household help, when he got there. The footman who'd answered his knocking led Longarm to an empty front parlor and told him to wait while he informed the madame. Then he lit out before Longarm could ask his permission to smoke.

So he was on his feet, admiring some coaching prints along one wall, when an imposing silver-haired madame indeed came in, wearing black silk and real pearls and saying she was Elsbeth Fraser but that her kid brother, the senator, had said he'd be back by now and ought to be showing up any moment.

She waved him to one of the two sofas facing each other near a fireplace filled with summer roses instead of winter coals, and took her own seat across from him as she demurely promised tea was on the way.

It would have been impolite to refuse. There was no mystery as to where all this soft living had hit her. You could see she'd never been more than plain, and now she had a rump to rival a Shetland pony and a chest that would do a drum major proud.

He silently warned his fool self to stop comparing tits and asses as he felt the old gal out on how much the senator had told her. As he learned she knew about as much as *he* did, Longarm loosened up and gave his real reason for coming over so late.

She rose to go open a drawer of a sideboard across the parlor and haul out a bundle of letters held together by an India rubber band, saying, "These all seem to have been written by the same hand, Deputy Long."

She returned to hand them over as she resumed her seat. He'd hauled out the letter Kate Thayer had received by then. So he was comparing the handwriting as another manservant came in with tea—the only choice being sugar or not, with no cream—and a sensible choice of slightly sweet Scotch short-bread or plain old scones.

He indicated no sugar as the old gal poured, musing, "Same handwriting. There's only one thing about it that stands out at all."

She finished and put the pot down, asking, "What might that be? It seems a rather unremarkable Spencerian script to me."

He nodded and said, "Thank you, ma'am. I've been trying to recall what they call that standardized handwriting they've been teaching since high schools were made free most everywhere right after the war. Spencerian, you call it?"

She nodded. "After P.R. Spencer, the noted educator who died during the war. I'm not sure how. He devised that clear and well-rounded script, with an even slant to the right, as a standard most pupils find easy to master as well as easy to read."

Longarm nodded. "My schoolmarm back in West-by-God-Virginia taught us her more old-timey way. It's lucky I've learned to hunt and peck on the typewriter for my official reports. I suspect the hand that wrote these letters learned a less-standardized way of writing before he, she, or it got to high school. There's more than one way to form some letters. A heap of old-timers write their small letter R to look sort of like a tight V, while most, including

53

Professor Spencer, seemed to favor an R that looks more like a butte against the skyline."

Elsbeth Fraser asked him why he thought of the letter writer as a he, she, or it.

"Because I don't know who wrote these, ma'am. Whoever it was used the more old-time letter R, no matter what Professor Spencer said. Crosses a T at the end of a word in a different way as well. By whipping the pen up and around to cross the T without lifting it off the paper, see?"

She took one envelope in hand and studied it with a slight frown as she murmured, "Jay-Jay was right about you. I never noticed that, and I once taught school while putting my baby brother through law school back in Indiana. My Lord, that seems like another world as well as a world away. Would you like a sample of *my* handwriting, Deputy Long?"

He chuckled. "Not hardly. I do mean to go over a heap of handwriting, unless I get lucky sooner. But I'm fixing to be mighty surprised if it's anyone your brother's known for long. Personal enemies seldom wait till a gent's serving his third term in the State House to start dropping him notes."

They heard a slight commotion out in the hall, and Senator Fraser came in to join them, saying, "There you are, Longarm. I was just now speaking of you with one of those policemen following me all over town!"

His sister smiled up at him like a doting mother with a tolerant attitude towards some sort of mischief as she asked, "Did they follow you too closely for you to steal even one kiss, Jay-Jay?"

The senator chuckled. "Nobody could follow me *that* close." Then, noting the confused expression on Longarm's face, the older man laughed even more boyishly and explained. "I've been sparking my true love, the distinguished Fionna Dunbar."

Longarm mentally added stinking rich to distinguished, but never said it. Another young widow left well off by

54

her husband had pointed out the plumper but attractive Widow Dunbar to him at the opera one night, and warned him to stay away from such a man-eater. It was rumored her late husband, the mining magnate Angus Dunbar, had sent all the way back to the old country for her and died of a heart stroke within a year of their wedding. Longarm was sure the senator knew that. He found the notion interesting himself. For while most men dreamed of the gal who could screw them to death, they never seemed to meet her.

Not wanting to talk about the senator's love life, Longarm explained why they had all his mail spread out on the table. Fraser thought that made sense but opined, "Chasing off to Texas after musters of old rebel raiders strikes me as a grand way to leave my flanks exposed, Deputy Long. I thought Marshal Vail had detailed you to protect me."

Longarm nodded and said, "That too. But do we wait to see if John Wilkes Booth gets past the guard at Ford's Theater, or do we find out he's staying at Surratt's boardinghouse and grab him before he can hurt anyone else?"

The senator grimaced. "I saw what happened this afternoon to poor Durante. But doesn't that mean the maniac has to be up here in Denver, not down in Texas?"

Longarm nodded gravely. "Yep. But we don't know *where* in Denver. And we don't have the least notion what the killer looks like even if we did know where. But I know, or suspect, I'm on the trail of someone who learned one kind of handwriting as a kid, and was taught that Spencerian hand in high school after the war. It shouldn't take me much time in Texas to find out whether anybody in a five-man diamond patrol left any orphans the right age to fit that suspicion. Given the names of even a dozen such kids, how many high schools could I have to go to Texas?"

Fraser made a wry face. "Hundreds? You're talking about the biggest state in the Union, you know!"

Longarm said, "I only have to ask at school boards I can match up with the names of recorded war orphans. Sibley recruited all his raiders from west of the Brazos as well. So that cuts out a heap of populous East Texas school boards. I know what I'm doing, sir. I know Texas Rangers as well as other Texas pals I can call on for help. I doubt it would take more than a few days to either cut me a trail leading back to Denver or eliminate that lost patrol entirely!"

Elsbeth Fraser looked confused and asked, "Didn't you just tell me you thought rumors about the final fate of those missing Texans formed the basis of all these wild accusations, Custis?"

Longarm shook his head. "No, ma'am. I said it was possible. Not even the Confederate vet who told their tale on paper claims to know a blamed thing for certain. There's no telling what other rumors have been floating around for years. It's possible the letter writer's kinsman was killed by a cannon ball, or was never killed at all and just ran off to California instead of going home to support a wife and kids after the war. That happens after every war as well, you know."

He got to his feet, adding, "Meanwhile, it's just as possible the letter writer never lost a daddy in any war. That happens too. But we have to treat the threats as real. So I'd best get cracking."

The lady of the house chose to show him out. He didn't know why till he wound up alone in the vestibule with old Elsbeth. She didn't exactly pin him to the wall in the dimly lit semi-private space. But he couldn't have gotten past her without shoving against her big old tits. So he never did as she told him, "Don't leave town, Custis. That madman could be right across the street this instant!"

He said soothingly, "Not without discussing it with the copper badges over yonder, ma'am. Sergeant Nolan has your back alley entrance covered, and come morning, Deputies Smiley and Dutch will be covering the senate floor from above with repeating rifles and a stern view of political assassination."

She was actually leaning against him now. It didn't hurt. But it sure felt silly. She insisted, "Stay here tonight. We've plenty of room, and you could leave with Jay-Jay in the morning after a grand breakfast."

He insisted, gently but firmly, "I got other places to go tonight, ma'am."

He'd meant that. For one thing, he had to go down to that livery on Tremont and square things with the night crew whether that pony had made it back to her stall or not.

But being a woman, even one that old, she said, "You single men are all alike. But what if I could show you how to combine business with pleasure, or some fun in bed, while you guard our very lives?"

He could only hope she had some serving wench in mind. He sure as hell didn't want to have fun in bed with any of the manservants he'd seen, and that only left her.

He pushed by, seeing she was going to rub her big old tits against him either way, and insisted he was still on duty. So she let him go with a sad little sigh. It wasn't till he'd strode a full block that he began to wonder if he'd missed out on anything good.

Chapter 6

That bay had made it back to the livery, and they'd been more worried about Longarm than pissed at him there. So he had a few at the Black Cat, and then ambled on home to his hired digs across Cherry Creek to spend the rest of the night in bed alone. It happened that way now and again.

Next morning he treated himself to a more thorough bath and shave, put on fresh linens, ate a decent breakfast, and showed up at the office to ask Billy Vail's permission to leave town for just a few days.

Henry said the boss hadn't come in yet, but nodded at a pasteboard box full of musty papers. "Smiley dropped this off for you. Said to tell you they were carbon onionskins and we don't have to give them back."

When Longarm asked to whom, Henry explained Smiley and Dutch had stopped by Guard Headquarters after the senate knocked off for the day around four and requested all the wartime musters of the Colorado Firsters. When Longarm chuckled and said he'd heard Dutch request things in his own persuasive way, Henry nodded and said, "They'd already made sure Troopers Fraser and Thayer had ridden with the outfit when Dutch had the notion you might as well have it all."

Longarm asked where the helpful deputies were now. Henry said they had the morning shift up at the State House, while Gilmore and Davis would be covering the senate floor that afternoon.

They were jawing about the best train connections to Austin when Billy Vail grumped in to tell Longarm, "I just had breakfast at the Palace with a mighty pissed-off state senator. You're invited to noon dinner with him— same place, same time as yesterday, he said. What's this shit about wanting to run off to Texas on him while his assassin is here in Denver?"

Longarm replied soothingly, "Give me a couple of days in the old Confederate files down yonder, and I may know better where the son of a bitch would be holed up here in Colorado."

Vail growled, "That's why Western Union was created, you footloose rascal. Give Henry here a list of all the shit you need to know in Texas, and we can wire some old pals of mine in the Texas Rangers, at day rates, if you think that'll help."

Longarm shook his head and insisted, "You're as bad as this one old gal at the public library. She keeps asking me to tell her which books I want to look at so's she can fetch 'em for me and save a heap of pawing through her stacks. She can't seem to savvy that I *have* to paw and poke back there to see what they got before I know what I *want*. Dutch did right in hauling all this onionskin paper back with him. I know ninety-nine-and-nine-tenths percent of it ain't worth ass-wipe. But you never know what's there before you look. There could be another cuss named Fraser who rode with the Firsters at Glorieta, for instance."

Henry said, "Dutch says there were several, Fraser being a fairly common name if you're Scotch. But none of them work as well as Senator Fraser for executing prisoners. One was a color bearer, one was a mess sergeant, and—"

"I'd rather see for myself," Longarm cut in, putting the books he'd brought up from the watchman's desk atop the papers in the big heavy box. "A grudge-holding war orphan could have confounded Fraser with a similar name, such as Fleishman or Frank, or who knows what I'll find before I find it? Meanwhile, I don't see how a Texas war orphan could have been going through the Union records of the Colorado Firsters until damned recently."

Henry brightened and suggested, "Hey, what if we looked into all the young Southern jaspers who've asked to see old militia records since the President relaxed the rules keeping old rebels in their proper places?"

Longarm shook his head. "Too many faces and likely fake names for any disinterested armory clerk to remember with any sure accuracy. After that, he'd hardly find anything about the butchery of that lost patrol in files *we* can't find it in. If it's written down anywhere that anybody executed them Texicans, it'll likely be in a Texican file. I won't know till I poke around whether General H.H. Sibley was professional enough to keep an order-of-battle file. Both sides came out at the end more professional than they were when they got into it. But you'd think a man would have to know something of soldiering before they made him a general."

Vail said grudgingly, "No order-of-battle book would give the name of enemy troopers. But finding a noncom named Fraser or something close might help. I want you to keep that dinner date and clear it with the senator, though."

Henry offered to get to work in the meantime with the railroad timetables in his own office files.

So that left Longarm free to haul everything into a side office and get dust in his mouth poking through one damned tedious roster after another before he leafed through those damned Stratton books again in search of anything he'd missed.

He hadn't missed anything. He noted exactly which troops Kate Thayer's father, the senator, and everyone with names at all like them might have served with at the time that rebel patrol got lost. Nobody seemed to work better than anyone else. So he could have said he'd come in that horny old widow in vain if it hadn't felt so good, or if a good lawman didn't know eliminating facts could help as much as *finding* something. He now knew, for instance, that nobody had based serious accusations against any Colorado Firsters on anything to be found in the Firsters' own wartime records.

He felt as if he needed another bath, but settled for a whore bath before leaving for that eatery up by the cathedral.

As he strode into it, hat in hand, he didn't see the senator at any of the tables. A picture hat with a stuffed egret atop it and a well-stacked redhead under it called him over to a far corner. He knew what the famous Fionna Dunbar looked like, and the senator had told him she was his true love. So he was more chagrined than surprised when he joined her and she told him Fraser was at some meeting, and that his sour-faced secretary had told her the senator would meet his true love and his bodyguard at the restaurant as soon as he could break free.

It would have been rude to tell a lady he wished her beau hadn't told the whole blamed State House where he'd be at high noon. So he just sat down and asked her how much the senator had told her about the mail he'd been getting.

The handsome but sort of horsey redhead in the big hat and green bodice a size too tight for her heroic chest said her Jay-Jay—as she called him too—had told her all about the death threats and warned her she might not be too safe in his company for a spell. Longarm decided he liked her better when she added, "None of us will ever get out of this world alive, and a politician who hasn't got anyone sore enough to want him dead just hasn't been doing his job. What do you think we should be drinking while we wait for Jay-Jay, Custis?"

He suggested the house wine, knowing she'd look unrefined with a beer stein in front of her, and figuring a place that served so many priests would likely have decent wine.

She nodded and he caught a waiter's eye. She seemed surprised when Longarm knew what the waiter meant by Chablis. He didn't brag about the fancy places he'd been to in the company of other wealthy widows, some of them better-looking and most of them younger.

He figured she was around forty, and even though you'd never know it from her manicured hands and cared-for eyebrows, he suspected she'd slopped a hog or more in her younger days, before she'd met the right folks. But he didn't ask her if she'd heard how one could marry more money in a day than most could earn in a lifetime doing anything else. He figured she likely knew it.

The waiter brought the white wine in the bottle and uncorked it. The wealthy widow seemed as surprised that Longarm knew how to go through the bull of trying one sip and then allowing that he and the lady would accept the wine. He'd often wondered what they'd do if you told them it was shitty vinegar and you didn't want *none*. But only kids and yahoos such as Dutch ever acted up like that just to prove they saw through all the fancy manners.

He'd have rather have had a good lager, but it wasn't bad for white wine and she was sport enough to say so, even though she was no doubt used to dining fancier, judging by the hint of double chin under her still-smooth oval face. As they chatted in the meaningless way of society swells who didn't know each other well, he noticed she'd worked hard on her diction as well as her nails and eyebrows. There was just a hint of heather in her modulated tones. She'd swapped her original Scotch burr for an upper-class British accent he doubted old Queen Victoria in person could have managed. She likely didn't know she was using some of the fancier words wrong. Longarm knew better than to tell her. But a country boy who liked to read knew lots of fancy words and what they really meant.

He knew she'd have felt dumb if he'd assured her she didn't have to put on such an act with him. He knew she thought her act fooled everyone. He wondered how the senator's big sister, being a former schoolmarm, kept from laughing. Thinking back, though, old Elsbeth hadn't low-rated her kid brother's true love. So maybe she saw the brassy but unsure redhead's good points too.

They'd only finished their first servings of white wine when they were joined by Senator Fraser. He pecked Fionna on the cheek without getting poked in the eye with an egret plume, and shook with Longarm as he told them both he was sorry for keeping them waiting.

He was explaining about some political powwow in the senate cloak room when that waiter came over and they ordered their dinners.

So it was over the soup of the day, which was black bean, when the older man got around to asking Longarm if he still wanted to go on a mad dash to Texas.

Before Longarm could reply, the senator reached inside his frock coat to haul out an envelope. "This was in my morning mail when I got to my office," he said.

Longarm set aside his soup spoon and took the latest death threat for a look-see. It looked like all the others, save for the postmark. The message was the same. The writer was fixing to avenge Dear Daddy and those other innocent Texican scouts any minute now.

Knowing the lady across from him was in on the game, Longarm gave the letter back, content to note, "Nobody can accuse the cuss of a flare for originality, Senator. You noticed the postmark, of course?"

The man the mail had been addressed to nodded. "Naturally. It was sent from somewhere right here in Denver!"

Longarm got back to his soup. He had no call to worry the older gent needlessly, and it was interesting he didn't seem to know that latest one had been postmarked at the Capitol Hill branch office a hop, skip, and jump from the State House. It might be even more interesting to notice whether anyone else paid attention to such details.

As the waiter was taking away their soup plates Longarm explained to them both how he'd finally managed to find some names that seemed to go with West Texas boys who'd never come back from the war.

He got out his notebook and read them off to the senator, who swore he'd never heard of any Corporal Alcott, and that none of those other names meant toad squat to him either.

Longarm put the list away, explaining that Texas likely knew them far better. "Governor Gilpin and his Colorado Volunteers never got to put together a rebel order of battle before the rebels were in Santa Fe and bound for Pikes Peak. So our best bet would be any Confederate files still on hand down Austin way. Now that they're allowed more bragging about their noble lost cause, they've taken to putting up zinc statues and calling every ex-private in Hood's Texas Brigade a colonel. Old guerrillas who rode with outfits such as Sibley's only call themselves Confederate captains."

Fionna Dunbar dimpled and said that reminded her of Scottish chiefs. Senator Fraser asked what an order of battle might be. It was easy to forget they didn't tell enlisted men about such matters as a rule.

Longarm said, "I only learned about such staff details after I got out and read up on what all that noise had been about, sir. Intelligence officers, if that ain't a contradiction in terms, like to try for lists of enemy units, including their organization and roll call whenever possible. It's surprisingly possible when a good staff man knows how to use scouts, spies, and talkative prisoners."

The redhead asked what use an enemy roll call would be to officers who never got to order them around.

Longarm explained, "Orders of battle, as they call such lists, can come in mighty handy to a commander planning what to do next, ma'am. As an easy example, Union General McClellan skunked Robert E. Lee at Antietam, but he didn't know it. Boys in butternut gray lay dead in piles from The Cornfield to The Bloody Lane, but McClellan had lost a lot of boys in Union blue and had no idea how many men Lee had left. So he pulled in his horns and snatched defeat from the jaws of victory by letting a whipped and dispirited enemy army limp away, lick its wounds, and regroup."

As he saw she understood, he added, "General McClellan designed a swell cavalry saddle. I use one myself. So he might have done better in the battle that ruined his rep if he'd had a better grip on who and what he was up against. By the end of the war most outfits were keeping orders of battle on all their opposite numbers."

The senator frowned. "Are you suggesting a glorified bandit like H.H. Sibley kept a roll call of the Colorado Volunteers?"

Longarm chuckled at the picture and replied, "I doubt he had more than a rough tally on his own ragged rascals, sir. I'm going to feel a heap more respect for him if he left any records worth pawing through at this late date. But my point is that nobody in Colorado seems able to tell me who that letter writer's dear old dad might have been. As of now we only have five possible names. It shouldn't take long to find out whether anyone in that one lost patrol left an orphan who'd have been the right age then and now. I want to make certain those five were the only ones who were never accounted for, in case nobody from that lost patrol pans out, see?"

The redhead said she did. That may have been why the senator let go a weary sigh and allowed that Longarm might know best about his own trade.

So after the waiter brought their main courses, they just ate them without arguing. The senator allowed that he knew about Gilmore and Davis replacing the morning shift that afternoon, and agreed it might be unwise to attend any public social gatherings for a spell. His Fionna blushed becomingly for such an old gal when her swain winked at her and said they were planning on dining in that coming weekend.

Longarm didn't ask whether they meant to sleep at her place or his. The Denver P.D. could watch either as well, once they'd been tipped off discreetly. He made a mental note to mention it to Billy Vail before he left for Texas that afternoon.

He'd feel silly as hell if he came all the way back from Austin to find the no-longer-young but sort of sweet-looking couple dead at the hands of that crackpot, who had to be right there in Denver even as they ordered dessert.

Chapter 7

The first capital of Texas had been the awkwardly situated town called Washington on the Brazos. They soon moved it to Austin, at the center of things, where the flat farming country of East Texas meets the more hilly cattle country of West Texas at the Rio Colorado.

Neither the state of Colorado nor the more famous and bigger river originating in and named after Colorado were anywhere near Austin. So it took Longarm a tedious thirty-six hours to get there by rail, counting layovers at transfer points too short to check into a damned hotel but far longer than anyone wanted to read magazines and sit at coffee counters in damned depots.

Hence Longarm was travel-weary, red-eyed, and unshaven on the last leg of his long train ride between Fort Worth and the state capital. His one good suit of tobacco brown tweed might have been black with locomotive soot by then if he'd been wearing it. But the fussy dress code of the current reform Administration hardly extended to a deputy on the road, as long as nobody in Washington was watching, so he'd put on a hickory work shirt and the faded denim jacket and jeans he liked to wear out on open range. His fancier duds were rolled in his bedding, lashed to the skirts of his old army saddle, across the well-packed saddlebags. The saddle, with his Winchester '73 booted to it, rode ahead in the baggage car, checked through to Austin by a well-traveled man who knew better than to run after trains with a loaded-down saddle when he didn't really have to.

He'd ridden partway free with a courtesy pass, and wrangled a Pullman bunk for half price from a conductor he knew. But past Fort Worth he was on his own money. So he was watching the sun go down, again, from an unpadded seat in a third-class coach car of the MKT Line as he neared the end of the bodacious trip. He was saving himself almost four cents a mile of his six-cents-a-mile travel allowance, and was enjoying the jerking and jolting more than the bedraggled young mother in the hard seat ahead of him. She'd got on at Waco with her two kids, a whining little gal of around four and a snot-nosed boy of five or six. Neither kid had gotten any better behaved in the two or three hours since. Longarm was tempted to lean forward and assure the drab blonde they were almost there. But she'd likely suspect he was trying to start up with her. You could see she'd been the sort of gal men got fresh with once upon a time.

The snotty little boy had discovered Longarm's gun rig during a thoughtless stroll by Longarm to the pisser at the rear of their car. But Longarm didn't want to let him hold it, and said so, not unkindly, when the kid peered over the back of their seat to ask without saying please.

His mother's neck got pink under her upswept but disheveled straw-colored hair as she softly warned her brat not to bother the gentleman.

The kid said, "Aw, Mom, he ain't no gentleman. He's a cowboy, and he won't let me play with his gun like Uncle Ray does."

It wouldn't have been polite to call anyone's uncle a total asshole. So Longarm just said, "My gun's loaded, sonny. But I'll let you hold my badge for a minute if you promise to give it right back."

68

The kid did, of course. So Longarm got out his wallet, unpinned his federal badge, and gravely handed it over the back of the seat. The little gal wanted to hold it too. The boy wouldn't let her, and asked his mother what the writing said.

The back of her neck got really red as she almost whispered, "It says U.S. Deputy Marshal, Jimmy. Now please sit still and let Little Sister pet it before you give it back to the nice gentleman."

The kid didn't want to. Longarm growled, "You heard your mother, Jim. Let Little Sister see it too, or I'm taking it right back!"

The kid did. The little gal called his badge a "Piddy" and kissed it. Both adults had to chuckle. The drab blonde was almost pretty as she half turned to hand his now-sticky badge over the seat-back to him, blushing becomingly as she murmured, "You do have a way with children, sir. How many of your own might there be at home?"

He followed her drift. He assured her he and his wife had five of the little rascals, three boys and two gals. That sounded about right to him, and assured her he wasn't a lone wolf on the prowl for married-up but unescorted women. So they got to talking about her man who'd be waiting to meet her and her train-weary kids in Austin.

He'd noticed the trouble she'd had getting on back in Waco with the kids and two good-sized carpetbags. So he pointed up at the overhead luggage rack with his chin and assured her he and old Jim could likely manage her bags if she'd just hang on to Little Sister.

She said she didn't want to put him to that much trouble, and asked about his own baggage. He explained he'd checked it through and told her, "I'll just see you and your load as far as your man and such transportation as he may have waiting for you all. Nobody but me can get away with my old McClellan and saddle gun without presenting my claim check. I sometimes leave things overnight in

69

railroad baggage rooms and I've seldom lost anything that way."

So she just argued enough about it to be polite as they slowed down to roll into Austin rail yards in the tricky gloaming light. Then they stopped, and he got down her baggage as if he owned it, telling her boy, "Jim, I want you to help me by hanging on to this one leather handle with me whilst your mom walks ahead with Little Sister. They know better than me what your dad looks like, see?"

So once they got lined up better in the aisle with all the others getting off, things worked out pretty good, and in point of fact far better than Longarm knew at the time.

For the hired guns laying in wait for a tall lean cuss in a brown tweed suit with matching Stetson and mustache felt no call to pay any attention to a harrassed-looking cuss dressed like a cowboy, herding what had to be his wife and kids off the same train while wrestling with their baggage.

The tall Texan inside the waiting room gave Longarm a more concerned look before his young wife and small daughter ran forward to grab hold of him. The little gal only said, "Daddy, Daddy, Daddy!" but the wife told him Longarm was a lawman who'd been kind to them on the train. So the two men shook on it, and the gent said he had a buckboard out front and could manage from there. So they shook on it again and parted friendly.

Longarm started to go get his own baggage. Then he had a better idea. He figured he'd save lugging shit around Austin in the evening rush if he checked into a hotel for the night and then went back for his gear, once he knew where he wanted it.

Austin wasn't all that big and he'd been there before. So he knew most everything of any importance would be an easy walk from the intersection of Seventh Street and Congress Avenue, near the fairly wide river. He found a side-street hotel which he remembered was a tad closer to the library and historical society sharing the same city block a tad to the northwest. Neither would be open at this hour, but steps saved were steps never wasted come morning, so he asked at the desk and they had a room on the third floor for hire at six bits a night—if you were willing to use the washroom down the hall. He took it, pocketed the key, and said he'd be back sooner or later with his baggage. The clerk didn't care. He made guests pay in advance with or without baggage.

But it was early of a balmy evening. The night was young and so was Longarm. He'd walked some of the stiffness out of his long legs, but still felt restless after that long train ride on his rump. He'd eaten along the way, so many times he didn't feel like he'd ever want a ham on rye or a glazed donut with coffee for as long as he lived.

But a nice cold beer sounded tempting, after that orange soda pop he could still taste. So once he got back to the depot he strode for the taproom instead of the baggage room down the other way. The beer on trains tended to be warm as well as expensively bottled. But they assured him at the bar of the railroad station's taproom he could get cool draft, piped up from kegs packed in wet gunny sacking down in their dank cellar. So he allowed he'd try a schooner.

The taproom was never deserted, day or night, in a world that ran on steam that was never allowed to cool off. But naturally, between trains, things got much slower. Some traveling men and the sorts of tinhorns who lived off the traveling men were playing cards at a corner table. A more experienced traveling man was nursing a beer and reading a dime novel at another table. There were two gents bellied up to the bar within earshot of Longarm. He wouldn't have strained his ears so hard if their conversation hadn't sounded so urgent.

They were both dressed for riding, though a mite self-indulgently for dollar-a-day hired help. He figured them for foremen or trail bosses if they really herded Texas stock

71

for a living. They were both well heeled with low-slung double-action six-guns—a Colt much like Longarm's own in the case of the shorter and older-looking one, while the taller and younger one favored an S&W. Longarm saw both packed "Russian" ammo in the cartridge loops of their gun rigs. That was something to inspire a man to listen in as they had a few serious words with their mild drinks. The "Russian" was a wildcat round designed at the behest of some Russian duke for a Cossack weapon with a bit more punch than the common and reliable .44-40. It threw a slightly longer slug with a slightly bigger charge of powder in its slightly longer brass. Most plain old American shootists had about the same use for the .44-Russian as Longarm. The slight improvement in striking power hardly made up for needing two whole sorts of ammunition for your side arm and your .44-40 saddle gun. Such wildcat brass might be all very well for Cossacks who packed guns for their old Czar, but nobody in the American West had much use for it . . . save for show-off kids and those few professional gunslicks who felt they needed every bit of edge they could get.

The two grown men talking just down the way didn't strike Longarm as show-off kids. He managed to edge a bit closer without being too obvious, but it still strained his ears to make out: "I still say he came in on that last train or an earlier one. What's his army saddle doing in that baggage room if it wasn't him as left it there?"

The other one was closer. But it evened out because his back was to Longarm as he replied, "Longarm ain't the only cuss who ever bought a McClellan after the war cheap. I tell you there was nobody answering to his description who got off that last train from the north. So never you mind whose saddle that was you saw. If it's hissen, it ain't going nowheres till he shows up."

The first one protested that there wouldn't be another train from the north for hours. Longarm didn't want to wait that long either. But he took his time and drank some more beer before he called out to the barkeep in a desperately casual tone for directions to their gents' room.

The barkeep said they didn't have one, since their customers were free to use the one attached to the waiting room just outside. Longarm considered, decided there was no better way, and told the barkeep to watch his beer because he was only going to water his boots.

The archway out to the waiting room felt like it was miles away, and his spine tingled under his denim jacket as he casually strode that far with his back to the hired guns.

Then he was out in the waiting room still alive. He didn't have to piss. He swept the crowd for some Texas law. He didn't see any. He took a deep breath, turned around, and drew his .44-40. There was just no better way to take even one of them alive, and dead men told no tales about who'd hired them. So he strode back in, six-gun leveled, in hopes he'd gotten the drop on them with his simple ruse.

It hadn't worked as Longarm had hoped. Men who live by the gun soon learn every simple ruse. Longarm would never know what he'd done to make the older one spook. He only knew that as he came back in they were both facing his way and the older one had already gone for his own gun.

Nobody fooled around with .44-Russian Double Action, so Longarm shot to kill and did so, downing his man with a plain old .44-40 over the heart. He tried to be gentler with the other gunslick, but even shot in one hip, the stubborn cuss kept trying to draw. So Longarm had to fire again, gut-shooting him to knock all the fight out of him, but still hoping for some conversation.

He kicked the man's gun under the brass rail along the base of the bar and stood over them both, reloading, as a couple of railroad dicks came in, their own guns drawn, demanding some damned explanations *poco* damned *tiempo*, as they said down Texas way.

73

Longarm called out, "I'm the law, federal. I was just about to ask this poor dying rascal why he and his dead pal were planning to do much the same to me."

The one nearest his feet on the sawdusted tiles protested weakly, "We never meant you no harm, you gut-shooting bastard! It was a pest called Longarm in a sissy suit we'd been hired to stop!"

Longarm hunkered down to gingerly lift some bloody shirtfront a bit and whistle softly before he said, "You found him, and vice versa. You were wrong about my traveling duds, and lucky for me, neither of you knew my face as I walked past you with a family not my own. But we digress, and if you'd like me to notify any kith and kin you can commence by telling me who you were in life, and who hired the two of you to gun a stranger who'd done you no harm!"

The hip-shot and gut-shot gunslick groaned, "They called me Grat Jones up in Waco where my true love, French Dorothy, should be waiting on word of my fate in Madame Lunette's. For she may have been a soiled dove, but French Dorothy and me were different."

Longarm said, "I'm sure she loved you best. Who was your pal and who were you both working for, damn it?"

The gunslick croaked, "Call him Bobwire Joe, and he was the one as made the deal for us. I never met the gal he said wanted Longarm—I mean you—put down for treating her mean."

One of the railroad dicks asked mildly, "You get some gal in that much trouble, Longarm?"

Longarm said truthfully, "I don't know. Ain't been down this way all that recent, but a gal that sore at me might have been willing to hold a grudge quite a while."

He nudged the shot-up killer on the floor and demanded, "Were the two of you hired in Waco or somewhere else?"

The gunslick didn't answer. Longarm moved his own gun muzzle near the blankly staring eyes, holstered the gun, and felt the side of the downed man's neck before he muttered, "Shit, for a professional tough he sure died easy. Either of you boys ever hear of a Waco whore they call French Dorothy?"

One of them said, "Nope. But Madame Lunette's place is a notorious house of ill repute near our Waco depot. They serve the transient trade more perverse transgressions than your average workingman can afford."

The other one brightened and volunteered, "Oh, you mean that whorehouse that puts on the animal acts for the edification of traveling men on expense accounts?"

Longarm said he followed their drift and added, "I'll look up old French Dorothy on my way back. Got to change trains in Waco in any case. Meanwhile the Rangers are likely to want a full report on this mysterious shootout."

Neither volunteered to go fetch the Rangers. They seemed to feel it was Longarm's case entirely, since he'd shot both rascals and they'd heard the one confess it had been Longarm they'd been after.

So Longarm rose back to his considerable height and growled, "All right. Make sure nobody moves either body till I get back with some Texas law."

He started to say something else. Then he decided it made more sense for him to hunker back down and lift both dead gunslicks' wallets than it might to tempt others with such suggestions.

Chapter 8

There was nothing like gunning total strangers in a rail-road depot to spoil any plans a man may have made for his first evening in a strange town.

His fellow lawmen understood his position, but not even he was able to explain how he'd ever wound up in it. So Longarm spent a good three hours jawing with the Austin P.D. and the Texas Rangers.

The Rangers asked the most questions. Organized back in the '40s to fight Comanches and malcontents out of Mexico, the Texas Rangers had been disbanded by the victors after the war and replaced by the unpopular Texas State Police of the Reconstruction Era. Now that President Hayes had ended Reconstruction in the former Confederate states, the Rangers had come back, with a vengeance, to assume the duties divided between the state guard and state police in most of the rest of the West. Longarm got the impression they resented a mere federal lawman messing with homegrown Texican murderers as he told them about those threatening letters and the killing in Colorado of that Pinkerton man by a self-styled war orphan from their Lone Star State.

The Ranger captain in command at Austin allowed that Longarm was free to poke through all the old records he liked, as long as it was understood that Texas would worry about questioning whores in Waco.

It wouldn't have been polite to ask whether a madam who ran a well-known house of ill repute, featuring performances of bestiality for the amusement of customers too drunk to get beastly, called for a payoff to the state law, the local law, or both. So Longarm gravely agreed it might be best if Texas asked their own French Dorothy who in blue blazes the late Grat Jones had really been.

The Rangers, in turn, agreed to share such shit with a federal man if he agreed to keep them up to date on anything new he dug up on the ill-fated Texas invasion of New Mexico, Sibley never having made it to his chosen target of Colorado. None of the Texicans he'd talked to so far in Austin had admitted to having taken part in the raid.

More than one seemed old enough to have fought for the Lost Cause. But Longarm didn't press it. He'd often found it best to disremember which side he'd ridden for, and the winners never had recovered all the U.S. Treasury notes from the many banks the retreating Texicans had robbed on their way home.

The Austin P.D. was agreeable about the dead gunslicks, once Longarm had agreed they'd best take custody of those expensive guns and some of the money he'd found in their well-stuffed wallets. He told himself it was only fair he hang on to some silver certificates, at least until he could jot down their serial numbers for future reference. The Austin P.D. said they'd bury the brutes in Potter's Field down the river, unless some kith or kin came forward to claim the bodies and answer a heap of questions.

So Longarm wound up in bed alone at his hotel, being too romantic by nature to settle for anything he could hope to pick up by the time he was done signing statements for half of Texas in more than one damned smoke-filled room.

But at least the next morning he was up early, cold sober, to consume a light breakfast of *tamales y frijoles con huevos revueltos* at a hole-in-the-wall café he'd recalled from an earlier visit. The *enchilada* who served him was prettier than the fat old gal who'd been there the last time. But he just left her a whole dime so she'd remember him as fondly, and moseyed over to the historical society down the block from the main library.

A hearty old gal of, say, forty, with henna-rinsed hair and a hefty laugh, said she'd be proud to show him all they had on General H.H. Sibley's near-conquest of Colorado. As he followed her back through the stacks, noting how heroically *she* was stacked, she confided that her Uncle Seth had ridden with the West Texas Brigade when she'd been but a wee one. Longarm was too gallant to tell any lady older than him he'd been big enough to join up at the time, after fibbing a mite about his date of birth. He knew a gal who'd been older than him at the time Sibley's guerrillas had had their great adventure could be a font of information if he played her right on a free-running line.

He didn't lie. He told her who he was. He just left some things out when she put two and two together and figured out he was doing military research, now that everyone was on the same side again and there was no telling when Texas and the U.S. Army might have to invade Mexico again and teach that sassy El Presidente Diaz some proper manners.

He gravely agreed the ungrateful greaser ought to remember who it was that saved his country from the damned old Frogs by ordering Louis Napoleon to withdraw his French Foreign Legion and let Juarez and that so-called Emperor Max just shoot it out.

The big old Texican lady got down a weighty tome, saying, "This would be as total a roll call of the West Texas Brigade as we have on hand back here, Deputy Long. As you'll see, it's set in print from the somewhat uncertain handwriting of many a company clerk. So a lot of the names could be spelled wrong or left out entirely."

As Longarm took the load off her dusty hands she added, "We get a heap of old rebels in here who swear they rode with Sibley but can't find proof in any records now. Some of 'em might even be telling the truth."

Longarm smiled thinly and said, "I've heard some mighty odd figures on both sides since anyone was writing 'em down when all of us were more young and foolish. If half the men who now say they rode with the Colorado Firsters had even been out this way, then none of Sibley's raiders would have got away."

She warned, "Bite your tongue and don't ever call the West Texas Brigade *raiders* in any part of Texas. Some of the enlisted men may have been uniformed sort of informally, and they're still arguing over whether General Sibley held a real commission, like the more famous General Hood, but my Uncle Seth's bullet scars were real enough and I'll not have him mean-mouthed, hear?"

Longarm led the way back to the reading tables as he said soothingly, "I heard *Hood*'s Texas Brigade charged through fire and salt at the battles of Gaines Mill, Chickamauga, and Franklin."

She beamed at him. "You heard right. My *Daddy* rode with John Bell Hood, and died a hero's death for Texas at Franklin along with half a dozen Confederate generals and no fewer than fifty-four colonels! The Yankees shot the liver and lights out of us at Franklin, but in the end that blue-bellied and yellow-livered Schofield retreated all the way to Nashville!"

She didn't sound all that upset about her father considering, and that was something to study on. Placing the heavy tome on an oakwood reading table, he turned to her and cautiously said, "I've been looking into the case of another child of Texas who lost a father to the North, ma'am."

She said, "Call me Billie. Everybody does, and what's *your* handle—aside from Handsome, I mean?"

He laughed and said he'd answer to Custis if she promised not to laugh. Then he said, "Getting back to serious stuff, Miss Billie, do you find it odd that someone who says he or she lost a father in that war might still have it in for the very boy in blue who may have done the dastardly deed?"

She frowned thoughtfully. "You mean personally? How? I don't have the least notion who put a minié ball in my poor daddy's breast in the hills of Tennessee. I know it must have been *some* Yank, and I sort of hope somebody got him in that same battle. But to tell the truth, I don't lose sleep over a faceless wonder I wouldn't know from Adam if I woke up in bed with him!"

She fluttered her lashes and looked away as she coyly added, "Not that I wake up in bed that often with total strangers, you understand. I was brought up quality and have to really know a gent before I let him hold my hand!"

He said he could see that. So she punched him on the arm, warned him not to think he could talk his way to bed with her, and left him to go through the old company rolls.

There were more than enough of them. Sibley's Brigade had been organized along dragoon or mounted infantry lines, with three or four companies to a battalion, four battalions to a regiment, and five regiments plus artillery and service units to a brigade. He read the table of contents in the front, and learned that a small cross by a name meant the cuss had been killed, while C meant sick or wounded and M meant missing in action or deserted.

There were as many of those as crosses. Longarm wasn't surprised. A dirty little secret of the War Between the States, and likely a heap of other wars, was the number of men on both sides who'd simply lit out when the going got too rough for them. Desertion was easy in the fog of warfare, and few records had been complete, even at the time.

Nobody would ever know exactly how many, on both sides, had simply floated with the tide of battle to be slaughtered like dumb brutes, or come out the far side as a vet who'd seen the elephant and would never tire of boring his grandchildren with those war stories everyone seemed to tell.

Longarm couldn't find anything about a five-man diamond patrol being captured and executed by Chivington's Four Hundred. He couldn't even locate any Corporal Lew Alcott among the rebel Major Pyron's men—and hadn't Pyron been the Texican directly opposing the outfit old Senator Fraser had been with?

Longarm kept at it, spitting paper dust and wishing he dared to smoke amid all those mummified records. It wasn't easy, but at last he found a Corporal Lew Alcott, in the scout platoon of H.Q. & H.Q. Company of Sibley's main column.

But that didn't seem right. As Longarm had read before, Sibley had seized Santa Fe and, holding it with about two thousand of his men, had dispatched his Colonel W.R. Scurry over to the Sangre de Cristos, with the eleven hundred riders the Union Colonel Slough would tangle with at Glorieta Pass.

So how could Senator Fraser, or anyone riding with Chivington under Slough, be remotely responsible for the death of Alcott and his boys if they'd been back in Sibley's Santa Fe headquarters at the time?

Longarm noted a cross next to Alcott's name and home address. Now that he knew where to look he soon found Billy Bascom and Hank Masters as well. Both names had small crosses, with no other comment. Longarm wrote down the three home addresses given, noting the corporal had hailed from San Antone while the other two had been off spreads in nearby Medina and Frio Counties, or about as far west as Texas cow country had spread before the war. Nobody but Mexicans had taken cows as seriously before the war as they'd have to after it.

Longarm still didn't like what he'd found so far. He put the heavy tome back where he'd found it, and scouted up the fake redhead to ask if her society had more about the sort of complicated fight up around Glorieta Pass.

She had more than he had time to deal with. The Texas Historical Society seemed to be of the opinion Texas would have won the war if only that sissy from Virginia hadn't given in at Appomattox so soon.

He'd already read some of the bragging tomes. But he skimmed through them some more to make certain he hadn't missed any names. Sibley's wild but not impossible grab for the Colorado gold fields had wound down in a running gunfight from Glorieta Pass, through Santa Fe and down the upper Rio Grande, till Sibley's shot-up brigade had split up in an every-man-for-himself run for home north of El Paso. A man who knew something about tracking across paper could save heaps of page-turning by consulting the indexes in the backs of most history books for the names he was after. But if anyone had seen fit to record the final fates of Corporal Alcott and his pals in any detail, it hadn't been by any of the main authorities on the losing side. That fatal little cross meant Alcott had never made it home, and had been listed as killed in action or dead from any of the other causes of death in such a downright unhealthy war. Longarm had read the Union Army had lost far more men to agues than shot and shell. The Confederate records were less complete. Their ambulance corps had been also. So it was safe to say Sibley had lost between six and eight hundred men in scattered firefights, and Lord only knows how many might have just up and died along the way. So Alcott, Bascom, or Masters might have been killed by snakebites or bad falls as far as anyone in Austin could prove. But when he asked the fake redhead, she confirmed his sinking suspicions they'd have more complete records at their branch at San Antone.

The first time he asked about orders of battle he had to explain, and she thought keeping a roll call of any enemy outfit sounded sort of silly. But upon reflection she did recall they had heaps of handwritten documents in San Antone. She said they even had last letters home from old boys who'd died at the Alamo, on both sides.

Then she said it was going on noon, so she'd have to lock up for a spell. But she invited him to come home with her for dinner so he could get an early start that afternoon, after she'd served him up some real Texican hospitality.

It was a caution how bold gals got as they got too old for most men to whistle at them. Longarm suspected both phenomena had some connection. Ladies collecting dust in libraries seemed to get even hornier than schoolmarms as their dull days added up to dry celibate months, or even years if they didn't watch out.

She wasn't bad either, but there were times a man had to choose between his duty and his pleasure when he had a train to catch, and she wasn't downright beautiful.

So he regretfully declined her kind offer and strode back out into the noonday glare, grateful for the wide brim of his Stetson even as he wished it was wider.

He checked in at the Ranger station before wasting five cents a word at Western Union on questions they might be able to answer by this time.

They could. The Rangers up in Waco had inspired Madame Lunette to recall she did indeed have a French Dorothy somewhere around her premises. French Dorothy, in turn, had finally managed to recall a "hopeless case" who'd told her he loved her from head to toe, albeit mostly in the middle. French Dorothy had assured the Rangers she'd warned Jones his favorite way of displaying a heap of devotion was against statute law in Texas, and she flatly denied any knowledge of other crimes he and his pal, Bobwire Joe, might have had in mind.

Another soiled dove who'd known Bobwire Joe better confirmed the tattoos the Austin coroner's office had already noted. A dagger through the eye of a skull, a mermaid in a Comanche war bonnet, and a lump in one thigh that came out as an old .54-caliber minié ball added up to the Rangers as one William Kruger, an unreconstructed rebel fired by the Thompson brothers after a couple of cattle drives for mistreating men and killing cows.

Longarm agreed a hand would have to be poison mean to get fired by Ben Thompson for Gawd's sake. The Ranger going through the files with him allowed that Kruger had been accused of worse things than riding ugly through Dodge of a Saturday night. It hadn't been proven, till the night before at the depot, but old Kruger had been known far and wide as a man whose gun could be hired by the hour. But seeing that he'd tried to draw on a U.S. deputy marshal in front of witnesses, it would never have to be proven now. The younger cunt-licker had been an obvious hired gun no matter what his real name had been.

That still left who'd hired them, and why. The Rangers were inclined to accept Longarm's notion that no whore-house madam in Waco had ever been sore at him. He, in turn, agreed few whores paying protection money as it was would want to jeopardize their standing in the Waco community by aiding and abetting anything more serious than crimes against nature.

They shook on it and parted friendly. Longarm stopped to replenish his supply of cheroots at a tobacco shop across the way, and then he headed over to the Western Union. Their front door was mostly glass. As he admired his own tall approach he noticed that a gent who'd been in the tobacco shop seemed to be following him. There wasn't much he could do about a cuss crossing a public thorough-fare in broad-ass daylight, and anybody had the same right he did to use the facilities provided by Western Union.

But it was better to feel safe than sorry. So when the stranger came in after him, Longarm bellied up to the counter to ask the clerk if they might be holding any tele-grams for Mort Morrison, foreman of the Diamond K.

The Western Union man said they weren't. Longarm would have been surprised if they were. Mort Morrison worked on the Middle Fork up near Boulder, and the Diamond K was a horse spread just outside of Denver. The denim-clad deputy sighed, said something about Uncle Dan being a tight old bastard, and moved down the counter to rip off a telegram blank and commence to block out a message to his home office.

The stranger who'd entered after him, of middle age and dressed more like a preacher or whiskey drummer, seemed to have changed his own mind about sending a wire. As he left to resume his post across the street, Longarm slid his message along the counter and told the clerk, "I'd like this sent at night-letter rates. For as you'll see when you repeat it in Morse, it's only a progress report and to tell the truth, I ain't been making much progress."

The clerk glanced down, blinked, and asked, "How come you just told me you were a ranch foreman if you're really a U.S. marshal?"

Longarm replied, "I'm only a deputy marshal, reporting to the U.S. Marshal Vail this night letter's meant for. I wasn't fibbing to *you* just now. I was fibbing to that off-duty undertaker who seemed a tad interested in another man's beeswax. Was he anyone we know?"

The clerk shrugged, "Never saw him before. Before today, I mean. I've been wondering why a man would come in, more than once, and then leave without saying or doing anything. It ain't as if we put on puppet shows in here, you know."

Longarm got out two cheroots and handed one across the counter as he mused, "*His* silent pantomime could be intended to meet up with someone other than old Mort Morrison, from the back. I'll ask him. Meanwhile, might you have any wires for me in my own right, as Deputy Custis Long?"

They did. But as in the case of his own progress report, the wire Henry had likely sent only told him nothing much seemed to be going on back home. The Colorado Senate had adjourned for a longer weekend than honest workingmen got. Meanwhile both local and federal lawmen were sticking tight as ticks to Senator Fraser, who'd taken to wearing that old Navy Colt under his prissy frock coat.

Longarm put the wire away and made sure he had five in the wheel of his .44-40. Then he took his double derringer off one end of his watch chain, made sure it was loaded—even though he'd done that, as usual, when he first woke up—and palmed it in one big hand before he stepped innocently out in the noonday sunlight to cross the street in a desperately casual manner.

But when he got to the impassive wooden Indian out front of the shop across the street, took a deep breath, and glanced casually inside, he saw the mysterious cuss in the rusty black suit had lit out. There was no way to ask the son of a bitch whether he'd lit out because he figured he'd overstayed his welcome at both the tobacco shop and Western Union, or because he'd not been fooled by that charade across the way.

Longarm studied all the window glass he passed on his way back to his hotel. Nobody seemed to be tailing him. But you might not have to tail a target if you knew which way it was headed.

He'd just wired Billy Vail he was headed for San Antone, and why. He hadn't told anyone at that Ranger station. Had he mentioned going there to that big fake redhead at the historical society?

It hardly mattered. She'd be home having her noon dinner just now, and Billy Vail wouldn't get his progress report, sent at night-letter rates, until Saturday morning. Maybe Monday morning if the wire wasn't delivered before noon. Meanwhile, the railroad timetable he'd read that Friday morning said there was a southbound local leaving for San Antone around one in the afternoon. So he could make it if he got a move on, and it would be interesting to see who else moved fast in the midday sun of high summer in Texas.

Chapter 9

San Antone, called San Antonio by Mexicans and other outsiders, lay two hours by train and a mite further to the southwest in its attitude. For if Austin was the center of things in Texas, San Antone was the center of things in Texas cattle country.

Things hadn't been planned that way by humankind. As a man with a secret vice called reading in bed, Longarm had long since concluded the Lord wrote history with a sly sense of humor. Having been there before, Longarm knew how a Mexican river crossing called Buxor had been taken over by Spanish missionaries bent on saving Comanche souls, and when that hadn't worked, converted to a northern outpost of the new United States of Mexico.

Caddo could be converted and Comanche held at bay by 'dobe and black powder. But the new government of Mexico was worried about El Pulpo del Norte, or Los Yanquis, to be polite. So some Mexican genius had a grand notion his countrymen were never going to forgive him for.

As a result, other Mexican congressmen agreed that it made sense for them to set up a buffer zone of English-speaking fellow Roman Catholics between themselves, the Comanche, and those mostly Protestant Yanquis with their dangerous notions about pursuing happiness west.

So they ceded generous grants of Comanche land to the Austin boys, land speculators of the Papist persuasion, with the understanding it would be parceled out to downtrodden Papist refugees from Yanqui Protestant persecution. Somebody down Mexico way had missed the proud signature of Charles Carroll of Carrollton, an Irish Catholic, on the Americano Declaration of Independence.

Meanwhile the Austin boys had lots of land to sell, on a first-come-first-served basis, so nobody asked and nobody would ever know how many of the original Texas Anglos had been Catholic, Protestant, or perhaps of the Hebrew persuasion. English-speaking white folks faced with dusky furriners in a new land had enough to worry about without arguing religion. So the next thing Mexico knew, it had a vast northern province filling fast with folks who sure looked gringo, sure talked gringo, and sure acted gringo. So they passed some laws to make the Texas settlers act more Mexican, and Texas naturally declared its independence, with a good many Hispano-Texans agreeing it was a grand notion.

The Mexican President-Dictator-General Antonio Lopez de Santa Anna, who would one day introduce chewing gum to the gringo market, but not just yet, stormed north to slaughter some gringo upstarts, but mostly got his ass whupped at San Jacinto. So they were still talking about the heroic but hopeless stand gents like Bowie, Crockett, and Travis had made in San Antone, fighting for their God-given rights to Life, Liberty, and the Peculiar Institution of Chattel Slavery.

As everyone knew, the notion of being a Texican had been born in the funeral pyres of the men who died fighting at the Alamo. But the Lord had written on with his tongue in his cheek and some mighty fickle weather above the marginal rangelands of West Texas. For the sons of the Southern planters who'd come west to spread Dixie into another brand of country entirely had grown up to be Texas buckaroos, as the Anglo tongue coped with the Spanish word *vaquero,* or "cowboy."

It had taken Texas some time to see this. So despite the little West Texas had in common with the Old South by the time of that War Between the States, old General Sibley had somehow convinced thirty-seven hundred Texicans, mostly cowhands from around San Antone, to ride with him to that fateful fight at Glorieta.

Longarm was only interested in the small handful who'd ridden into something even worse with the late Corporal Alcott.

First things coming first, a man getting off the day-tripper from Austin had to consider getting about such a sprawled-out city under a mighty unforgiving Southwest sun. So he toted his loaded-up saddle across to the livery nearest the railroad depot in hopes of finding a stout enough pony for hire.

The elderly gent in charge was less surprised than Longarm as he nodded and said, "We been expecting you, Deputy Long. It ain't for me to say, of course, but if you'll trust the word of a man who's been to Dodge and back on horseback, you'll let us fix you up with—"

"Hold on," Longarm said. "Who told you my name and that I was coming here? I didn't know I was myself when I first got up this very day!"

The hostler said, "His name was Martin, Marvin, something like that. Said he was working with you in the same trackdown and described you to cross every T. Said you were tall and dark with a mustache and gun-muzzle gray eyes. Said you'd be wearing a dark brown hat crushed Colorado-style, and that you favored a McClellan saddle and Winchester '73. Are you saying you're another U.S. deputy entire?"

Longarm grimaced. "The question before the house is whether someone who knew I was coming baked a cake or had something else in mind. Forget what I just said about hiring a livery mount, old son. I got some other errands to run afoot first."

The hostler didn't seem to care. Longarm lugged his load around a corner to get the hell off Commerce Street, where others might expect to see an unwary tourist. He followed the narrower Blum Street almost as far as the Alamo Plaza, but stopped short to check into a down-at-the-heels *posada*, or hotel, that took in Mexicans.

Anglo riders could stay there too when they hadn't been paid recently. So the sort of sullen but otherwise pretty *señorita* in charge of the dutch door that doubled as a room clerk's desk didn't act surprised till he told her what he wanted.

Like most of her Tex-Mex generation, her English was accented just enough to sound sort of pretty. "Let me get this straight," she said. "You don't want a room for you. You don't want a room for a friend. You want a room for your *saddle*?"

Longarm said, "This north range Stetson too. I reckon I'd best hang on to my Winchester, scabbard and all. My hat and saddle won't require room service, or even an entire room, come to study on it. I just need a place to store them for a day or so, see?"

She answered dubiously, "They would take up little room under my own bed, and I could use the money as well as the management. But for why could you not check your things at the railroad depot for free? Just tell them you will be back later, after you decided which train you wish for to take."

"I tried that once," he said, getting out his badge as he confided, "I'm on a secret mission for the government, ma'am. I have reason to believe somebody else may be out to drygulch me before I can get to where I got to go, see?"

She reached out to steady his wallet with the identification card on display under isinglass. She gasped, gaped up at him wide-eyed, and marveled, "You are the one my

90

people call El Brazo Largo! You are the one who helped El Gato, La Mariposa, and other rebels get away from that old devil El Presidente Diaz and his wicked *rurales*!"

Longarm grinned sheepishly and murmured, "Not so loud, *por favor*. Like I just said, I'm trying to travel in secret, *comprende*?"

She glanced around the dingy empty lobby and whispered, "*Sí, comprendo mucho*! You have my word ten cardinals of the Inquisition would never never get me to admit you were in town!"

She refused to take any money for hiding his baggage. But he did get to tote it inside for her. On second thought, she said, he should simply drape his saddle over the foot of the bed in her simple but tidy room with one shuttered window. By this time he'd had some second thoughts as well. So he left his Winchester for now, but put his hat back on as he explained, "I have some errands to tend at places they could well be watching. So I'd best come back and make some final changes later."

She took him gingerly by one denim sleeve, pleading, "Won't you let me get some of our own *muchachos* for to watch your back for you, El Brazo Largo ? I know what your kind thinks of my kind when it comes to fighting, *pero*—"

"Bite you tongue!" he said with a stern frown. "If you know me as a pal of your own El Gato, you know better than to say I've never seen a Mexican fighting man. La Mariposa sure kills *rurales* good too, even if she is a durned old girl."

The younger and somewhat softer-looking *señorita* here in Texas smiled radiantly up at him. "*Es verdad*, you are as nice as you are brave, El Brazo Largo!"

He said, "My friends call me Custis, and you are called . . . ?"

"Paloma. Is not my real name, of course. But I like it."

He didn't ask why they'd nicknamed her after a dove. He'd already noticed she had a light complexion for her kind, and while her hair was hardly light enough to qualify as palomino, that light a shade of brown was likely striking enough to her Mexican kith and kin.

Leaving his telltale baggage with Paloma, but still striding about in his familiar Stetson, Longarm went back to Commerce Street to drop by the Western Union and wire his home office a progress report. He told them to send it via night-letter rates, seeing how little progress there was to report.

Despite all that had been written about it, the old Alamo wasn't all that near the center of San Antone. Longarm strode west along the far busier Commerce Street to the main or military plaza, where they'd built the city hall, main library, and such around the palace of the Spanish governor, after taking that away from the Mexicans as well.

Longarm bought a hot tamale at a plaza stand, and asked directions to the historical society's San Antone branch. He polished off the hot tamale with some gringo lemonade before he went there. It was getting hot as hell out by then.

But the 'dobe walls and jalousied windows of the historical society made things more endurable indoors. The pleasant old gent in charge reminded Longarm of a bank teller who'd run off to be a pirate. For despite his snuffy-colored frock coat and wire-framed specs, the old librarian had a wicked saber scar down one cheek and his left forearm ended in a wicked steel hook.

They were able to shake with their right hands, though, and before Longarm could finish telling the old Texican what he'd come for, the man in charge of the books declared knowingly, "You want the home addresses of Troopers Masters and Wallace. Corporal Alcott's only daughter died of the yellow jack around back '74 or so. Neither of the younger riders, Bascom or McArtle, were married up. Jake Wallace left a girl child too. She's still alive, but busy raising a family over to Val Verde

County. So like we already decided, the two sons and one daughter of Hank Masters, a day's ride west, would be your best bet."

Longarm blinked in confusion. "If you say so. Anyone can see you've been at the very books I was looking for, sir. But did I hear you say you've just been over 'em with somebody else?"

The librarian nodded blandly. "A Deputy Marner. I put everything down on paper. Saves straining one's brain at my age. I got slashed by a cavalry saber near Nashville, you know."

Longarm nodded and said soberly, "Hood's Texas Brigade fought like tigers at Franklin, they say. But we were talking about a lost patrol from Sibley's Brigade, sir."

The old-timer snorted and shot back, "Shoot, us real Texas Cav lost more than twice as many men than Sibley ever led in his pathetical guerrilla band! Like I told that other lawman, the so-called Battle of Glorieta was more a gunfight betwixt half-assed militia and bandits. That's all Sibley was, you know. General John Bell *Hood* commanded the genuine troops of *Texas* in the War Between the States!"

The older man, who couldn't have been any kid in the war, stared through Longarm at other men he'd known one time as he softly added, "Got us just about annihilated along that bloody road from Nashville to Atlanta. That's likely why there's so many pissant irregulars these days, bragging on how they rode for the cause under guerrilla shits such as Sibley, Quantrill, or that blowhard Bean."

Longarm tried to steer the conversation back to the here and now. The old-timer said that other lawman had made mention of some Colorado lance corporal butchering a captured Confederate patrol. He insisted there was nothing about that in any of the books he had on hand. But he agreed the names mentioned in those threatening letters did appear on Texas casualty lists. Period. There was no documentation putting Bascom, McArtle, Masters, and

Wallace in any patrol led by Corporal Alcott, a head-quarters clerk who'd been killed well *after* the Battle of Glorieta during the fighting retreat from Santa Fe.

Longarm suggested, "Try her this way. Everyone agrees *some* Texican scouts were captured. A dozen or more at Pigeon Ranch alone. Drawing on my own experience with such adventures, it's customary to lie like a rug when you're captured, right?"

The old-timer said, "I surely did when I come to in that Union Army hospital with a pretty Yankee nurse washing my privates. You say you rode in the war, old son?"

Longarm nodded. "Never mind what I might have done in the war. Captured scouts, giving the names of men they knew to be safe in the rear, could have made pure hash out of some old battle reports."

The librarian nodded. "That's what that other lawman was saying earlier. He said that whether any prisoners were killed or not, the records might show they'd been captured, but never been exchanged or turned loose at the end of the war."

Longarm scowled thoughtfully. "I'd better ask someone who might have been closer at the time. You say that Masters spread ain't too far and that other jasper knows about it? I don't recall any Deputy Marner I've ever discussed this case with. You say he told you he was working on it too?"

The older man nodded blandly. "Mentioned you by name and asked if you'd been by yet. When I said you hadn't, he just laughed and said it didn't matter. Said as long as he had a general idea where you'd be head-ed he could always meet up with you in his own good time."

Longarm tried not to let his true concerns show as he got directions to the Masters spread along with a fairly detailed description of a somewhat older, shorter, chunkier cuss in a rusty black suit. He had no call to tell the old librarian that sounded like the mysterious son of a bitch who'd been lurking near the Western Union in Austin. So he kept the disturbing suggestion to himself. But it was disturbing as hell just the same.

Chapter 10

By the time he'd run a last few errands afoot it was after
five in the afternoon and not cooling off enough to notice.
But the bright blaze of the Southwest sun concerned him
more than its heat as he hugged the shadows of many
a side street all the way back to that small *posada*. He
made sure he wasn't being tailed before he turned the
final corner. He still glanced both ways, at nothing much,
before he ducked inside.

It wasn't quitting time yet. Hence, as he'd planned,
the dingy lobby was still empty, save for little Paloma
lounging at the double door. When he told her tersely, *"Lo
que necesito es mucho soledad!"* Paloma popped open the
bottom half of her Dutch door and sort of dragged him
inside, whispering, "Nobody would think to disturb you
in my room!"

He didn't argue. He told her along the way why he
thought somebody could be laying for him. Once they
were alone in her little bedchamber he explained, "I've
a new hat in this paper sack. I went over wearing it to a
livery on the far side of the river, to pay in advance for the
hire of a nondescript bay pony and a Texas saddle. I put
this Colorado-crushed Stetson on again before I bought
me another tamale at the plaza. Then I cut me a mess of

corners and ran through many an old alley on my way back here."

Paloma nodded soberly. But he saw she had no idea what he was talking about. So he smiled reassuringly and explained, "If I leave here after sundown, packing my Winchester but under a gray Texas hat, I may just ride on out of town, to the north, say, as some good old Texas boy bound for most anywheres but that Masters spread. Once I'm well out of town I can naturally swing west some more, and sort of drift over to visit the kith and kin of a long-lost rebel scout at an angle my pal in the gloomy black outfit wasn't expecting, see?"

Paloma clapped her small tawny hands and chortled, "*Si!* They told us how you evaded both Los Rurales and Los Yaquis on the warpath that time! It makes me feel so proud to know I too have been of even a little help to El Brazo Largo and La Causa!"

Longarm felt obliged to say, "Hold on, Miss Paloma. I never said I was doing anything for La Revolución this afternoon. I'm on a pure Anglo case in hopes of catching at least one gringo crook!"

She said it didn't matter. Anyone who'd helped her own brand of rebels in the past would doubtless help them in the future. He didn't think she'd want to hear what old Billy Vail had had to say about any U.S. deputies mixing into Mexican politics ever again. So he just told her he'd be much obliged if she'd hide him out there until after dark.

Paloma said she would, and suggested he get in bed and catch up on some sleep, seeing it wouldn't be dark for hours and he'd be out on the trail all night, if he had any luck at all.

He said he'd be proud to take her up on that. So she dimpled up at him and said she'd lock up and be right outside if he needed anything.

When he asked her to wake him around sundown, she assured him she'd do better than that. She said she got off duty at suppertime. So she'd bring him some *tortillas y frijoles* along with a wake-up cup or two of stout Mex coffee.

She did too. But first Longarm got to sleep a good couple of hours in her rough clean bed. It was rough because he found homespun cotton ticking over the corn-husk mattress under her monk's-cloth top sheet after he'd draped the wool blankets over his saddle down at the foot of the rustic bed. It was clean, like everything else Paloma tended, including Paloma, because that seemed to be the way she liked things. Once he'd shut the blinds all the way, he noticed the darkened room smelled more of beeswax and naphtha soap than the jasmine perfume she and so many of her breed seemed to fancy. He'd noticed both her low-cut white blouse and gathered print skirts had been freshly laundered as well.

That may have been why he was dreaming of that jasmine-scented Chin Ling at the laundry back in Denver, who seemed to be getting dirty with him and a hot tamale at the same time. He warned her, not unkindly, "It's the tamale you take in your mouth and my old organ-grinder you want up your ring-dang-doo, little darling."

The Chinee gal sobbed, with a Mexican accent, "Forgive me, I lost control when I saw you there with the covers down and your glorious erection so inspired and so tempting."

That was when Longarm opened his eyes to discover he wasn't getting a blow job from Chin Ling back in Denver after all. It took him longer to remember he was down in Texas than it did to realize he was a good ways up inside Paloma, as she went on playing stoop tag atop him with a tray of hot grub in danger of scalding either one of their chests as she tried to screw and balance his supper at the same time.

He grabbed the tray, saying, "Let me help you with that, and wouldn't you like to get undressed, Miss Paloma?"

She said he was so understanding as she peeled both her blouse and skirt off over her head without missing a bump or grind. Since he'd set the tray aside on a bed table by then, he reached up to haul her nude body down against his for some friendlier words.

She kissed back, friendly indeed, but protested it didn't go in her as deeply this way. So he rolled her on her back, hooked a bare elbow under both her naked knees, and proceeded to show her how a man could kiss sweet and hit bottom at the same time, if he put just a little thought and effort into his bedroom acrobatics.

Paloma sobbed that she'd never been screwed by such an acrobat in all her born days, and added she just couldn't wait to tell the other gals it was true what they'd heard about El Brazo Largo being *vero varon*!

He knew better than to beg her not to. Gents had as tough a time keeping the conquest of some famous gal to themselves, and nobody ever believed it when some trail hand said he'd been to bed with the Divine Sarah or Jersey Lily anyhow.

Once they'd both come, more than once, Paloma naturally cried, while Longarm sat up in bed to wolf down the bland but satisfying grub and perky black coffee.

He knew better than to ask any freshly screwed female what she was crying about. Some gals just did that, the way some gents just couldn't keep their eyes open afterwards.

He lit a cheroot to go with the last of the coffee, and leaned back on the pillows to cuddle her close and offer her an occasional puff. He didn't answer when she sobbed that she felt so ashamed of herself. So once she saw they weren't playing that game, she commenced to fool with the hair on his chest and ask what else he had in mind for the evening.

He figured he was good for at least one more shot up her sweet and spicy snatch. But he hadn't gotten his second wind yet. So he explained a bit more about the death threats to Senator Fraser. When she declared anyone who'd hold a grudge that long was *loco en la cabeza*, he considered the source and agreed, "We could be dealing with a festered brain. It gets even sillier when you can't find any proof of any such massacre in the official records kept by either side."

She asked how even a gringo could blame someone for something he might not have really done. He figured it would be more fun to screw her some more than talk about some vigilance committees he'd tangled with now and again.

So what with one thing and another, it was later than he'd first planned by the time he got back to that livery on the west side of town with his Winchester, saddlebags, and such. The older Mex still on duty opined he looked different in that big hat with its high crown creased West Texican. Longarm was more interested in whether anyone had been by to ask about anyone his size and shape wearing *any* sort of hat.

When the hostler assured him business had been slow since last they'd met, Longarm got out the written instructions to that Masters spread and read them off to the local rider.

The older man naturally said he didn't know anyone named Masters, but opined the country Longarm was headed into could be injurious to a stranger's health.

Longarm said, "I've already given you a bigger deposit than your fool bay barb is worth. What are they feuding about over yonder?"

"*Agua,*" said the Mex simply.

Longarm nodded and asked no more. Water rights were at feud in other parts. But nobody fought over water any harder than stockmen trying to raise beef on marginal range Mother Nature had designed with, say, jackrabbits or ground squirrels in mind. Water ran along the surface in many a West Texas arroyo some of the time. But cows eat grass when they're not drinking water. So the range within easy walking distance of public water tended to be grazed down to bare dirt. Water holes, or "tanks" in Texican usage, were usually claimed and fenced as private property, lawfully or not, and held for one's own stock against all comers no matter what their lawyers or hired guns might have to say about it.

The Mex at the San Antone livery couldn't say who the Masters family might be feuding with, or how seriously. So having helped him saddle and bridle the gilt bay barb he'd chosen earlier, Longarm mounted up to just go see for himself.

As he was riding out of the dooryard the old Mex, likely more worried about the pony, called something after Longarm about a trail town known as Halfway. Longarm knew where Halfway lay in relation to the Rio Frio to the west. Naming the place hadn't called for imagination. He didn't rein in to ask how come Halfway had a bad rep. Dinky trail towns that far from the nearest Ranger station could always get a mite mean in West Texas.

He rode off into the balmy night. Thanks to the quarter moon in a cloudless sky, it wasn't much darker out along the trail than it had been through the last few blocks of town. He could make out the dusty wagon trace ahead. He knew his mount would be able to see it by starlight if he didn't make it anywhere by moonset. He had to guess at whether they were growing beans or peppers in the fenced-in fields to either side. He could see the dark crops were too stubby for corn, and Mex farmers didn't grow half as much squash as their Indian cousins did. He knew those folks with a wistful lamp winking out at him from a distant window had to be Mex this far west. Anglo Texicans seemed to feel they'd been cut out to either sit on a plantation veranda or a cow pony. To hear some of them talk, it was a wonder they ever ate beans or drank liquor. For farm folks had to grow all that barley, hops, and such, once you studied on it.

He set an easy but steady pace, dismounting to rest his mount and stomp some blood back into his legs once an hour, and watering the pony every third stop. But by the time the moon was down and the sky behind him was pearling gray, he was mighty sorry he'd refused Paloma's kind offer of another hour's sleep after they'd done it dog-style that last time.

The livery mount was walking funny too, after a longer time away from its stall than it had learned to expect. So when it woke Longarm up by trying to bolt forward, he knew there was something ahead that a pony found tempting.

He let the bay barb have its way, seeing that was the way he was headed, and as they topped a rise at a trot he could make out a few pinpoints of light and a heap of dark rooftops ahead. So he knew he'd made better time than he'd expected. The pony, of course, was far more interested in the fodder and water it associated with the smell of any human settlement. So Longarm let it lope some, then reined in just outside the loose-knit sprawl of outbuildings. For a rider coming in at full gallop at dawn tended to unsettle folks this close to Mexico and more than one uncertain Indian nation.

He heard a blacksmith hammering, and followed the sound until sure enough, he located the town livery right next door. Others were up and about in the dawn's early light as Longarm dismounted in front of the livery. The smith, next door, stopped hammering and drifted out to have a closer look. Longarm suspected at first they just didn't have a whole lot to amuse themselves with in Halfway. But the smith turned out to be in charge of the livery and town corral as well.

Longarm wasn't ready to flash his badge or give his right name before he knew if anyone had been asking about him in these parts. So he said his name was Crawford, Crawford Long being the smart old doc who'd invented cutting off legs with ether just in time for the war. Crawford was also the last name of a pal who wrote for the *Denver Post*. Fake names worked best when you made sure you wouldn't forget them.

Naturally there was no way to ask if any mysterious men in black had been asking about a man wearing a fake name and a Texas hat. So Longarm declared he was on his way to that Masters spread a few more hours to the southwest, and the hostler-smith agreed his livery nag from San Antone seemed jaded. Longarm said, "I'm used to going longer without rest, and I'm sort of in a hurry. So what sort of a deal can you give me on the hire of a fresh mount, with this one here as its deposit?"

The hostler-smith pursed his lips thoughtfully and declared, "You must be in a hurry if you've ridden all the way from San Antone and still want to keep going. Why don't you have breakfast with us, out back, whilst we consider the future some?"

Longarm smiled thinly and asked, "And you wire the Rangers to ask if anyone's missing a gilt bay barb with that livery brand?"

The hostler-smith chuckled boyishly and said, "I see you're a well-traveled man. Come on out back and have some damned flapjacks if you ain't got a guilty conscience, Mister Crawford."

That sounded fair. So Longarm led the barb inside and helped with the unsaddling before he followed the jovial but canny businessman through a back door and across the backyard to a smaller 'dobe house.

There, a plump but pretty Indian gal seemed proud to serve him a heap of flapjacks, with black coffee he needed more, as he sat on the side veranda watching the sky turn pink.

The hostler-smith, in the meantime, got his busy self over to the Western Union relay in the back of their general store. As he asked the storekeeper-cum-telegraph-clerk to ask the Rangers in San Antone about that strange pony,

103

a strange rider who'd been lounging against another counter, sipping root beer, perked up to listen with interest.

Knowing it would take a few minutes to get any answer, the hostler-smith moved over to the pickle barrel and sat down. As his eyes met the stranger's the local businessman nodded and said, "I reckon I got time for a game of checkers if *you* have, Mister . . . ?"

"Call me Blacky," the stranger replied agreeably as he moved over to join the local by the pickle barrel. He waited until the man who'd wired the Rangers was setting up the checkerboard on a soap box between them before he casually remarked, "You say someone just rode into Halfway on a stolen horse?"

The hostler-smith shook his head and replied, "Wouldn't deal with a downright suspicious stranger. He looks all right. But you know what they say about it being better to be sure than sorry."

The stranger who called himself Blacky waited until they'd both made a few moves before he pressed his luck further. He let the older man jump one of his checkers and chuckle before he asked whether they might be talking about a tall drink of water riding a McClellan saddle under a dark pancaked Stetson.

When the hostler-smith shook his head and described a regular old Texas hand with a center-fire roping saddle and a regular Texas hat, Blacky threw caution to the winds and beat him easy so he could get back on his feet as well as on the prod. For he knew that infernal lawman Longarm would be along any minute if he was coming at all.

Chapter 11

That black coffee helped. It came as no surprise to Longarm that he wasn't wanted by the Rangers as a horse thief. The hostler-smith had no call to tell him about the checker-player in black who'd been asking about some other rider. So they settled on a spunky brown and white paint standing fourteen hands at her shoulder and reputed to be a tolerable cutting pony. Longarm had yet to have a livery nag described to him as only fit for the glue factory.

But Blue Ribbon, as she was called, got him on out to a sunflower windmill he'd been told to watch for in less than two hours. You could see the windmill, above a mesquite-covered rise, long before you got to see the spread it was pumping its tube well to water. A windmill tower tall enough to show above a swale surrounded by brushy rises all around had to be tall indeed. But Longarm knew they hadn't stuck it up in the sky like that to act stuck up, or even as a noted landmark. It took considerable wind to pump water this far from the Rio Frio, and the wind blew harder as you stuck things higher. As he swung a tad to his right to ride for the impressive tin sunflower, he figured that much mill would pump enough water for a small town or a big herd.

As he topped another rise, expecting to see the Masters spread at the base of the tall tower, he saw there was at least one more rise between him and that big windmill. An even bigger one than he'd first thought. Sizes as well as distances were tricky under the clear skies west of, say, Longitude 100.

Hence it took him a full second to realize that what looked to be a cow being chased by a cowboy over that rise was really a calf with a small kid tearing after it on a Shetland. The kid rode pretty good and had his throw-rope spinning dally-style. But Longarm could see the kid was too far back, by two lengths, when he let fly with his braided reata. The calf swerved to avoid the throw, short as it was. Calves did that when kids pestered them a lot. So Longarm saw the playful critter was headed his way, and having been a kid in his own time, he found himself shaking out a loop of the grass rope that had come with his hired stock saddle.

To hear that kid whoop in the distance, one would think he'd never seen a fool calf caught by a hind leg lest it hurt its fool self as it hit the end of the rope. Seeing he had a center-fire saddle with a dally horn, Longarm was able to spill the calf less roughly than they usually did north of the Staked Plains. Since the dally wasn't secured to the horn it was a two-hand job. So he kept backing his paint to keep the rope taut, with the critter spilt, while the kid dismounted to run on in and sit on the calf long enough to free its leg, calling out, "It's already branded, mister. I was only practicing!"

Longarm called back that he'd suspected as much, and proceeded to just haul in and recoil his rope as the kid and his victim both sprang up to head in opposite directions.

The kid remounted the shaggy brown Shetland and joined Longarm as he finished strapping the recoiled rope to his saddle swells. The kid exclaimed, "I've seen a Mex do that with a leather reata. But I've never heard tell of a white man who could roll a hoop of grass rope betwixt a calf's legs to trip it like so!"

Longarm said, "Well, I'm older than you, no offense, and there's still wonders *I* ain't seen. I'm looking for the Masters spread, pard."

The kid said he was Timmy Masters and that Longarm had found the place in time for dinner. Longarm knew it was too early in the morning for that, but he didn't argue. It was nigh impossible to visit a remote spread without getting invited for coffee and cake, or run off at gunpoint. Folks who took care of themselves out in the chaparral learned to take passing strangers seriously either way.

Longarm said to just call him Custis for now. He'd know soon enough whether he wanted to level with the kid's elders or not. Riding on in with the kid, he learned Timmy was the somewhat indulged child of the daughter of the late Hank Masters, and hence the grandson of a fallen hero of the Confederacy. But carefully clever questioning failed to cause the kid much excitement. Timmy knew about the War Between the States, but he had it taking place somewhere between the Battle of New Orleans and the Alamo, in the ancient times before his interest in roping calves. He knew his granddad had been killed by Damnyankees one time, when his momma had been a kid like him. But that was about the hair and hide of it.

Once they topped the next rise, Longarm could make out the whole Masters spread around the windmill tower and half-acre pond it was constantly pumping full of tube-well water. Travis and his men might have held off Santa Anna better out this way. For aside from all that water, the sprawl of Mex-style buildings had thicker 'dobe walls than the old Alamo. As they rode on down, Longarm casually asked the kid how come all the windows facing outward looked so much like rifle slits.

Timmy said, "We used to have Kiowa-Apache, even Comanche in these parts. Now we only have to worry about the durned old Cullpeppers."

Before Longarm could ask what a Cullpepper might be, a thick oaken door popped open down below and four grown men, one Anglo and three Mex, popped out to regard Longarm thoughtfully with their guns, a Winchester, a Remington, and two Spencers, held politely at port.

Young Timmy called out, "This here's my pal Custis, and wait till you see him rope, Uncle Chad!"

Longarm figured this was about time he told them who in blue blazes he was. So he did, and once they had it straight that none of the son-of-a-bitching Cullpeppers had gone to the law about folks who'd been there first, Chad Masters, the oldest boy of the late Trooper Masters, said to get right down and let the hired help care for his pony while he came on in for some West Texican hospitality.

So he did, and they turned out a likeable enough tribe as they fed and coffeed him. The younger Masters brother the librarian back in San Antone had mentioned was as dead as his late father, although not as mysteriously. He'd been killed by Comanches in his teens right after the war, as Texas was learning to drive its cows north to the rail lines and higher prices on the far side of the Red River of the South.

Miss Helena Brogan, nee Masters, was the matronly gal who owned up to Timmy while serving them her swell tuna pie, which was made with sweet cactus fruit, not fish, down that way.

She turned out to be the Widow Brogan, her man having died in a bad fall a couple of roundups back. So it seemed she and her brother owned the spread they'd been left by their folks. When Longarm followed up on that, as delicately as he was able, it was Miss Helena who said right out their pappy had been foolish riding off to conquer Colorado for the Confederacy like that with a wife, three kids, and a herd of his own to worry about.

Uncle Chad, who'd been about Longarm's age at the time of the war but apparently smarter about joining up, said they'd managed to hold on, thanks to their momma's head for business, three kids in their teens, and some faithful Mex help the Damnyankees hadn't set free on her after all. Chad Masters leaned back expansively to declare, "If the truth be known, we'd have been in a worse fix if it had been *Momma* who'd rid off with that fool Sibley insteady of Pappy."

His well-fed sister nodded, slicing more pie, and volunteered, "Pappy never would have cashed in on the rising beef prices after the war. Mamma always seemed to sense which way the wind was fixing to blow before anyone else could. Lord, I surely wish Mamma was here now. If she was, she'd know what to do about those carpetbagging Cullpeppers!"

That allowed Longarm to find out more than he'd ever really come to find out about purely local troubles. But the more they went on about their West Texas grass and even sparser water attracting too blamed many newcomers, the less likely it seemed anyone around there had been writing mean letters to a distant state senator.

Taking the bull by the horns, he cut into a tirade about idiots not understanding a tube well up a swale was hardly stealing surface runoff from any fool Cullpepper. "As a lawman who's had to arrest stubborn folks over water feuding, it's my educated guess your downstream neighbors could only take you to law with any hope of winning if they could prove in court you folks had dammed a stream that had been running across their land when they first bought or claimed it. Have any of 'em ever threatened you with anything meaner than a lawsuit?"

When Chad Master asked if that wasn't mean enough, Longarm shook his head and said, "Nope. Mean is writing threatening letters and following 'em up with murder. So I'd sure like to get back to your daddy's death up Glorieta way."

The only two survivors of Texas Trooper Masters exchanged what he took for sincerely puzzled glances before Miss Helena said, "We told you. Pappy was kilt in the war, and Mamma never forgave him. What on earth has the war to do with us today? It was years ago, when we were only kids, and as I just told you, we managed to make a go of it in the end."

Her brother nodded soberly and said, "We remember Pappy fondly, but if the truth be known, he wasn't half as practical as Momma. It was her notion there had to be water under this swale. Pappy never studied the lay of the land, save in hopes of striking color. So . . ."

"So *somebody* has been accusing a state senator of killing their dear old daddy in the war and I'm rapidly running out of somebodies!" Longarm declared. "Most of the others in your father's lost patrol left no kids to feel one way or the other about it. I can't see another daughter masterminding some black plot from clean out California way. So who's left?"

Chad Master said they didn't know what in thunder he was talking about. So Longarm had to go back over the whole dumb story again, and while little Timmy thought it was mighty mean of the Damnyankees to do his grandpappy so dirty, his Uncle Chad just agreed it was a dumb story. He sounded sure as he told Longarm, "The way *we* heard it, from a pal who was with him, Pappy took a minié ball in the head, south of Santa Fe, and never knew what hit him!"

Longarm stared thoughtfully at Miss Helena, who didn't seem surprised, as he muttered, "Hold on. You folks heard your dad was killed in that retreat down the Rio Grande, *after* Glorieta?"

They both nodded. He asked if they'd been told anything about the other members of that so-called lost patrol. None of the names meant a thing to the former Helena Masters. Her brother said he'd heard of Alcott, Wallace, and maybe Bascom. He'd never met any of their kin.

Then Timmy piped up, "I don't understand something. If my grandpappy was hit in the head with a minié ball during a big battle, how could anybody name the Damnyankee who done it?"

Longarm stared soberly at the boy and replied, "Nobody sensible could, Timmy. I was in a battle one time. It ain't that easy to say for sure you hit a man when it was you who fired at him. Gunning a prisoner would be one thing. Pegging a shot across a battlefield would be another thing entire. Yet somebody sure feels certain Senator J. J. Fraser shot your grandfather and four others at the very same time and place."

Chad Masters asked what the senator had to say about that. When Longarm said Fraser couldn't remember shooting anyone in any war, it was Miss Helena, the daughter of the Texan some damned body had shot, who gently suggested, "You said yourself nobody sensible would accuse any particular soldier of firing a particular shot in a battle. So isn't it possible you're dealing with a raving lunatic?"

Longarm didn't answer. It was the most sensible suggestion anyone had made so far.

Chapter 12

Livery mounts move faster toward their feed troughs if you let them. So Longarm made it back to Halfway before noon, and it was just as well. For he was starting to feel the effects of staying awake so long.

First things coming first, he returned the hired mare to the cuss he'd hired her off, and said he wasn't ready to take back the bay barb just yet. He asked about that telegraph connection, and got directions to the Western Union branch in their general store. He only toted his personal saddlebags and Winchester along for safekeeping as he made his way there.

There were a couple of gents dressed cow and playing checkers when Longarm strode in. They looked harmless enough if you discounted the effort they made not to look at him as he passed. As a rule of thumb, it was safe to assume a stranger was looking you over in inverse proportion to how hard he was staring your way. But small-town folks were always curious about strangers. Like that Professor Darwin had pointed out in his scandalous writings, modern man was descended from rougher folks who'd been careful about anything or anybody at all strange.

Longarm would have wanted to wire his boss in code in any case. It went with the job and wasn't hard. He addressed his message to Uncle Billy at the marshal's home address, and simply noted he'd consulted all the local docs about Aunt Martha's condition to no avail. None of them had ever seen anything like her mysterious malady. He added he'd been told of a specialist out California way, but thought it sounded like a long shot. Then he asked what his Uncle Billy wanted him to do, allowed that he'd wait there in Halfway till he got a reply, and signed it, "Your loving nephew, Little Crawfish."

He agreed with the grocery-clerk-cum-telegrapher that the reply would likely be addressed to a Junior Crawford. For he and his old Uncle Billy had all sorts of secret family jokes.

There was no argument about it taking an hour or more for any reply, whether the messenger boy in Denver hurried both ways or not. So Longarm asked if there was a hotel in their fair city, seeing he'd been awake a spell.

The helpful storekeeper told him they sometimes put travelers up for the night above the Travis Saloon just down the way. So that was where Longarm headed, and sure enough, a kindly barkeep let him fill up on the free lunch for the price of one beer, and had his swamper show Longarm up to one of the small rooms opening out on the balcony wrapped around the cavernous main saloon. The swamper, an old Anglo who said he'd picked up that gimp leg in the war, agreed the place was laid out like a New Orleans whorehouse they both recalled from more militant days. That was because the Travis Saloon had been a bit wilder back when the stagecoaches had stopped out front. As he handed Longarm the key, the old-timer sighed and said, "Ain't near enough visitors these days to keep full-time whores in business."

Longarm tipped him a dime anyway, and locked the door after him with a luxurious sigh. He hadn't known how weary he was until he saw how long it could take a tired man to go to bed. He draped the saddlebags over the foot of the pipe-framed bed, stood his rifle in a corner

113

by the one small window, and let most everything but his
.44-40 and the pocket watch chained to his derringer flop
to the bare floor before he flopped his bare ass in bed,
pulled the covers over him, and hit the pillows as if he'd
been poleaxed.

The next thing he knew, a fly was crawling over his
face and those deviled eggs he might have overdone were
repeating on him. So he sat up to belch better. Then he
noticed the angle of the sunbeams lancing around the
edges of the window blind, and reached under the pillow
for his watch.

When he saw he'd slept close to six full hours, he
resisted the grand notion of flopping back down by
swinging his bare feet to the floor and asking himself
if pissing didn't sound like an even better idea.

He didn't want to use the chamber pot under the bed.
So he held out long enough to get dressed, strap his side
arm back on, and lock up before he ambled back along the
balcony to where, sure enough, they had a flush commode
with a sink and running water. That swamper had said
business had been better just a few summers back.

He felt more ready for action after a good pee and a
whore bath at the sink with cold water but plenty of stout
brown soap. So leaving his baggage and Winchester in
his room, Longarm went downstairs, noting there were
more customers that late in the day, and strode back
to the general store to see if Billy Vail had wired any
orders.

Billy hadn't. The old wage slave was either spending
the weekend at his office desk, or he'd had to take his
old lady somewhere more sociable. But it was already a
little after suppertime. So maybe a reply would soon be
on its way.

Longarm headed back up the street in search of his own
supper. He figured a place serving such a good free lunch
could surely manage a sit-down meal that wouldn't stunt a
growing boy's growth, and when he said so to the barkeep,

he was told to go sit in a corner while they saw what they could do for him. Friendly words and an occasional dime tip could carry a stranger farther than making faces at folks.

So Longarm was seated with his back to a far corner and a big old card table in front of him, his gunrig out of sight, when one of those riders who'd been playing checkers at the general store came through the swinging doors, along with a tall drink of water dressed in a black Charro outfit with a flat Spanish hat and his Remington Rider Conversion riding cross-draw with its tailored walnut grips forward.

Neither glanced Longarm's way once, so he knew they had to be as interested in him as he was in them as they both bellied up to the the bar with their back to him, their casual eyes facing the big mirrors of the back-bar.

The flashy one's side arm belied his being a top hand showing off his extra ten dollars a month. His weapon was the expensively reworked implement of a serious shootist.

As one of the first double actions patented, back in the cap-and-ball era, the Remington Rider's self-cranking was foolproof as well as simple. Designed as a cavalry weapon during the war, the model had failed to catch on because its rival Colt's cap-and-ball revolvers had been faster to load despite a somewhat slower rate of fire in the end. Remington had often led the way against its simpler and hence often more reliable rivals. Thus, when metallic cartridges came out in the late '60s Remington had been first to switch, offering conversion kits for customers already packing their earlier models. Since the earlier cap-and-ball revolvers had perforce had bigger cylinders than more up-to-date six-guns designed from scratch, it was up for grabs whether that jasper in black was set to throw lead fast in .45- or .50-caliber. Meanwhile, it seemed only prudent for Longarm to get his own .44-40 out and have it sitting in his lap for now.

A sort of pretty but way-too-young Mex gal came out from the back with a tray for him. Aside from the chili con carne and coffee he'd asked for, they'd sent him some *tapas*, or Mexican surprise snacks. Each *tapa* looked like the same bitty envelope of tortilla dough. But you could wind up with a mouthful of most anything once you bit into one. The first one he tried was apparently filled with red ants. So he got to work on the chili first to get used to the pain.

They'd not stinted on the peppers in his chili either. Tex-Mex cooks seldom did. Grub cooled off a bit, north or south of Texas, as folks tended to forget the Alamo. He was enjoying his chili con carne and fixing to try another *tapa*, when a soft-looking cuss in a hardcase cowboy outfit loomed over him, uninvited, to announce he'd heard he was in town and that they'd better talk it over.

Since he'd addressed a man he didn't know as "Mr. Crawford" Longarm felt no need to correct him. He just told the cuss to sit a spell and speak his piece.

The stranger grabbed a bentwood chair from a nearby empty table and swung it around to face Longarm. But before he sat across from Longarm the stranger said, loud enough to be heard at the bar, "I'd like it distinctly understood I'm not armed, Mr. Crawford!"

Longarm washed down some chili with coffee left-handed, and said not unkindly, "That's all right. I am. Who are you and what's this all about, friend?"

The pudgy stockman sat down, gulped, and said, "I'd be Warren Cullpepper. I'm sure your employers, the Masters bunch, told you more than enough about me and mine."

Longarm managed not to laugh out loud. It wasn't easy. He popped a *tapa* made from chicken liver and hot lava in his mouth to feel a mite less amused, and gravely replied, "They did. But I don't work for them, if that's what you're worried about. Putting some cards face-up, it's true I was out at the Masters spread this morning. We did talk about their dispute with you over water rights. I gave them my

116

views on the subject and nothing was said about blood and slaughter. I told 'em there was nothing you could do to them, and vice versa, that would stand up in court."

Cullpepper didn't look convinced. He said, "Far be it from me to call any man packing both a Winchester and a Colt a liar. But Chad Masters dared me to my face to come and take their water if I thought I had any riparian rights."

"You don't," said Longarm flatly. He shoved the platter of *tapas* toward Cullpepper in an amiable manner as he explained. "Under common law and Texas statute, no landowner has the right to dam or divert a long-established stream running across his property if his downstream neighbors can show he's cutting off their traditional water supply. That grassy swale both you and the older Masters spread occupy in part ain't *got* no surface water running down it when it ain't raining, which means most of the time in West Texas. I already told Chad Masters and the Widow Brogan they'd have no right to build a dam upstream from you. But they showed no indication they were planning to. They got a swell sunflower windmill pumping ground water from Lord knows how far down. I suggest to sink your own tube well and cut this bullshit, hear?"

Cullpepper protested, "That's what the argument's about. We have drilled for water, in more than one spot. The dowser we hired says that big sucker up at the Masters spread is hogging all the ground water for miles!"

Longarm tried another *tapa*, seeing Cullpepper didn't seem to want any, and asked how many miles they might be talking about. When the newcomer to West Texas said his own spread was no more than six miles down the swale from that monster windmill, Longarm grimaced and told him, "Get another dowser. Or save your money and just drill deeper. There's got to be water down there somewhere. Both your spreads lie on low ground. The mesquite growing all around can't grow at all unless there's water within sixty feet of the surface. From the way the Masters mill is pumping, and the way the water sinks back into the ground without running nowhere, we're talking *water*, plenty of water for both of you, if only you'd use you fool *heads*. Did that dowser you hired stop drilling when he hit bedrock?"

When Cullpepper said of course he had, with the soil barely damp above it, Longarm laughed and said, "Bedrock down this way is limestone. Wet as a sponge once you drill into it a ways. What in blue blazes have you been watering your stock with up to now?"

The greenhorn started a long sad tale of hauling water from the distant Rio Frio or the closer but muddier Medina after a good rain. But Longarm stopped him and said, "Hang some crepe on your nose to show Chad Masters your brain's been dead a spell. Then tell him you're sorry you worried him over nothing and he might even lend you some drilling tools. I swear I don't see why folks have to fight over water and fence lines when they've everything from grasshoppers to locoweed to worry about out this way."

Cullpepper still asked him to swear he hadn't been hired to dry-gulch anybody. Longarm was tempted to tell him to take a flying leap at a rolling wagon wheel, but it seemed easier to simply assure such a simple soul he hadn't been paid to gun *him*.

Warren Cullpepper rose uncertainly and backed out, apparently a mite undecided. Longarm got back to his chili con carne as meanwhile, over at the bar, the one who'd spotted him in the general store asked his partner in a low voice, "What do you think, Blacky? He's the right size and build and they did say he might be headed for that Masters spread, remember?"

The gunslick packing the Remington Rider growled, "I remember the mention of a Colorado crush also, and take the wax out of your ears. Didn't you just heard that sissy whining about the Masters clan importing gunhands for some sort of water war?"

The less-experienced hired gun shrugged and insisted, "Sure seems an odd coincidence if you ask me."

Blacky said, "Nobody asked you. A trouble bunch like the Masters bunch is naturally going to attract all sorts of trouble. We'll keep an eye on this galoot. But I ain't gunning nobody till I'm sure he's the one I've been paid to gun."

Chapter 13

Longarm finished off his spicy supper with blandly sweet almond cake and plenty of black coffee, and faced an uncertain night. He took his time, left a generous fifteen cents for the pretty little serving gal, and tried the telegraph branch again after sundown. The pair of gunslicks who'd been watching him eat were too slick to follow him back to the general store. So Longarm was alone as he sat by that pickle barrel reading his message, or orders, from his Uncle Billy.

In the same half-joking tone Longarm had used, Uncle Billy allowed that Aunt Martha's female complaints could be all in her head, and turned thumbs down on consulting that other expert out California way. In sum, he wanted his wandering nephew to quit fooling around down yonder, and come on home to hold Aunt Martha's hand and keep the neighborhood kids from disturbing her.

It made as much sense to Longarm. But he lit a cheroot and just sat and studied a spell after putting his orders away. What Miss Helena had suggested about the threatening letters coming from a lunatic worked swell until one considered the murder of Detective Durante and those hired guns who'd come after him in Austin. This wicked old world had lunatics to spare, a heap of them homicidal, but a lunatic with known gunslicks on retainer? Gunslicks by definition were dumber than they likely thought they were. But hardly dumb enough to knowingly sign on with a certifiably insane mastermind.

He got up and headed back to the Travis Saloon to gather his things and settle up before he headed back to San Antone. For no matter what some mastermind had in mind, this excursion to Texas seemed to have been a wild- goose chase. Senator Fraser said he'd never executed any rebel scouts, rebel records said he'd never executed any rebel scouts, and the kin of the scouts Longarm had talked to so far had never heard of Senator Fraser.

"Them accusations were likely cut from whole cloth," he muttered to himself as he ambled along the plank walk in the tricky light just after sundown. The man in black keeping an eye on him from across the street couldn't hear, of course, as Longarm said out loud, "There's got to be a reason. Even if I was only out to spook old Billy Vail with a dumb letter, I'd still accuse him of something he might have done. I'd never accuse him of cheating on his old lady with some gal he'd never met in some whorehouse he'd never been in!"

He found the saloon crowded and the barkeep busy as hell with the after-supper crowd. So he went on upstairs through the blue haze of tobacco smoke to fetch his saddlebags and Winchester before he had to pester anyone for his final tab.

He hadn't left a lamp or candle burning when he'd locked up before sundown. So the soft light shining out from under the closed door was enough to fill a thoughtful man's fist with his six-gun. He gingerly tried the latch with his free left hand. The door wasn't locked. He opened it fast and moved in the same way, throwing down on the lady seated on the bed before he'd had a good look at her.

She was staring up at him owl-eyed, but otherwise she was pretty as a picture. At least a picture in the *Police*

121

Gazette, of an actress or opera star. But she was wearing a fringed buckskin riding habit, and her chocolate hair was pinned up under a vanilla Texas hat. So he wasn't surprised when she cried, "I see you know I'm Irene Cullpepper, but don't shoot! I swear I've come in peace to make you a better offer than those Masters people could!"

Longarm put his pistol away, noting his Winchester still stood in the corner where he'd left it, as he politely inquired what relation she might be to old Warren Cullpepper.

When she said she was Warren's sister, Longarm was too polite to say he saw no family resemblance. He kicked the door shut behind him and said, "Before we go into water rights, how did you get in here in the first place, ma'am?"

She explained she'd told the Mex serving gal she'd come to make a private deal with El Señor Crawford. Longarm didn't say what he suspected that Mex serving gal had suspected such a pretty gringa had in mind. He said, "I've already had it out with your brother, Miss Irene. I assured him he'd misread my innocent visit to the Masters spread, and offered him some helpful hints on getting along better with your new neighbors."

She looked as dubious as her less kissable but somewhat softer brother as she replied, "So Warren just told me. Why are you playing cat and mouse with us this way? Chad Masters warned my brother he'd hire his own outside help if we took him to law over his water hogging, and surely you don't mean to say you hadn't heard about my brother's visit to Lawyer Bancroft in San Antonio?"

Longarm smiled thinly and replied, "Your neighbors will snicker if you don't learn to call it San Antone, ma'am. As to taking anyone to law over a tube well drilled on their own property, I'm sure your Lawyer Bancroft already told you he didn't want to talk that foolish in any Texas court for any amount of money."

She sighed. "I told Warren you Texans would stand together against us. Would it do a bit of good for us to assure you we lost kin fighting for the South too?"

He smiled gently and replied, "Probably not, if I was who you seem to think I am and the eyes of Texas were really on you that intently. You must harbor heaps of mean thoughts if you really think everyone for miles around is out to get you. I told your big crybaby brother what I told Chad Masters. There ain't nothing worth a serious fight out your way. A shiftless water dowser lied about water to excuse his own laziness or ignorance. There's just no way any well a good five miles away can rob you of all the ground water you have coming. If it's there at all you only have to *drill* for it, see?"

She didn't. She stared soberly up with tears in her chocolate eyes as she declared, "I'll give you five hundred dollars not to kill my brother or burn us out, Mister Crawford."

He laughed incredulously and said, "Call me Custis, and I'll spare your lives and property gratis."

She tossed her hat aside and reached up to unpin her lush hair as she said, "Don't mock me. I know Chad Masters couldn't have paid much more than the going price. How much more do you want, if I'm willing to throw in . . . all I have to offer?"

As her long hair cascaded down around her shoulders Longarm sighed and said, "You know, some night when I'm all alone in a strange bed I'm going to call myself things I'd dast not say in mixed company. But I don't shoot fish in a barrel either and . . . I wish you'd leave them buttons alone, ma'am."

Irene Cullpepper went on unbuttoning her fringed buckskin shirt as she calmly belied her own blushing face by demurely replying, "I don't know the going price for this sort of unskilled labor. But don't you think I'd be worth more to you than the average trail-town doxy?"

Longarm nodded soberly and replied, "You'd doubtless be able to demand a hundred a night on a payday night in Denver or Dodge, Miss Irene. But . . ."

"Five hundred dollars and me, any way you want me to pleasure you," she declared, gulping bravely before adding, "Even if it hurts."

Longarm reached under his jacket as he softly replied, "You must be mighty fond of your brother, and I can see I'm damned if I do and damned if I don't."

As he got out his wallet she got all the way out of her fringed jacket, nipples turgid but blushing like a rose as she sheepishly confessed, "You'll have to show me how if you want anything as wild as I've heard they do in for in Paris or New Orleans. I was only wed a short time when my bridegroom suffered a heart stroke."

Longarm gazed in admiration at her firm but heroic bare breasts as he wistfully remarked, "I believe you, ma'am. Torn betwixt good reasons to work undercover and the perils of an overwrought imagination, I reckon it would be safer to prove I ain't a hired gun. But could I have your word my secrets would be safe with you and you alone?"

She finished unfastening her split riding skirts and let them fall around her booted ankles, lowering her lashes as she faced him naked as a jay in all her glory, saying, "Anything you say. But please try to remember I'm not very experienced at this sort of thing!"

Noting she had thick chocolate hair all over, Longarm gulped and said, "Aw, mush, have a look at my infernal identification," as he held his open wallet out to her.

Her chocolate eyes stared in total confusion at his federal badge and printed identification as he explained, "I was only out at the Masters spread on government business having nothing to do with you or your brother. As you can see, my name ain't really Crawford, but Uncle Sam and me would be much obliged if you kept that under your hat . . . if you'd like to put it back on, ma'am."

She was blushing from her nipples up now as she gasped, "Oh, my heavens, whatever must you think of me now that you've, ah, seen so much of me!"

He soberly replied, "I think you're mighty pretty all over, and I know I'm going to kick myself all the way back to Denver for not letting you think I was more ugly for just a little longer."

She laughed knowingly, but hunkered down to gather up her skirts, and that looked sassy too, as she demurely asked, "Why didn't you? I suppose I'd have been so relieved I'd have forgiven you, Deputy Long."

He sighed and said, "My friends call me Custis, Miss Irene. I'd best step outside whilst you finish putting your duds back on. For I don't know about you, but I find this mighty distracting."

She hesitated, let go of her skirting, and rose back to her feet as naked as Venus rising from the waves in Austin boots as she calmly replied, "I'm afraid I know what you mean about cursing oneself alone in bed, Custis. I suppose we've all passed up more temptations than we might have gotten away with if only we'd been a bit bolder."

He put his wallet away and got rid of his own hat as he moved a step closer, softly agreeing, "There's only so many grabs for them gold rings on a merry-go-round that don't go round forever. But did I mention I got to ride on forever no later than midnight?"

She stepped out of her skirting and moved to meet him in no more than her high-heeled boots, eyelids lowered but flushed face tilted up to his as she half murmured and half sobbed, "I don't care. I just want you to grab me now, Custis. I know all too well what you mean about lost chances and it's been so long, so many cruel lonely nights, since I've been . . . you know."

He took her in his arms and held her tight for a howdy kiss. She kissed back, desperate with desire, and he wasn't too surprised when she confided, as he lowered her to the bed, she'd been attracted to him when first she'd decided

125

to sacrifice her fair white body to an outlaw's lust to save her fool brother.

It was her own grand notion, the inexperienced thing, to wedge a pillow under her own slender hips as he popped more than one button shucking his own duds. So he paid no mind as she bit her lower lip and hissed in shock, or pleasure, when first he entered her. For as tight as she seemed, she was wet and hot with desire as he rammed it deep as it would go, and sure enough, she was soon hollering for more and he was mighty glad her boots weren't spurred as she locked her ankles around the nape of his neck, swearing she'd kill him if he ever stopped, or tried to leave her.

He could only hope she meant before she came. For Billy Vail's orders to get back to Denver seemed serious too.

Longarm rode off in the dark with a worried mind, knowing full well how promises made at midnight could be broken in the cold gray light of dawn, and that the swiftest means of communication known to man were telegraph, telephone, and tell-a-woman.

But by the time he changed trains in Austin the next day he'd decided it hardly mattered whether she told everyone back there in Halfway he was an outlaw or a lawman. For unless everyone he'd talked to down that way had been better actors than anyone had any right to be, this whole fool trip to Texas had been worthless.

He hadn't found a lick of evidence connecting Senator Fraser, or anyone else who'd ridden with the Colorado Firsters during the war, with any massacre of any lost patrol. Records kept by the side the dead soldiers had ridden for failed to show they'd ever been sent on any fool patrol in the first place, and at least two of the victims named had apparently been killed in other actions nowhere near one another.

As to concerns about the ability of a lunatic to recruit serious professionals, there was another way that might work. A worried mind could be connecting the dots the wrong way, to present a picture that made no sense because it wasn't sensible.

Any lawman worth his salt made heaps of enemies, and Longarm had made many an arrest and planted more than one badman in the ground down Texas way. So it was more than possible those others pests had never been inspired by that letter writer at all!

By the time he had to change trains again, at Waco, Longarm had bounced such notions back and forth, smoking many a cheroot while many a telegraph pole whipped past outside. They got into Waco just before suppertime, and the northbound Pullman he had to catch wouldn't be leaving until after sundown. So that gave him time to see what else someone might have told a woman if he skipped his supper in the depot beanery.

If San Antone was more cow than Austin, Waco was more farm. Built on the site of a wiped-out Indian settlement, but named after those Indians, even though the Mex spelling had been Hueco, Waco lay far enough up the Brazos from the original Texas capital for a railroad trestle across the fickle quicksandy river. This had led in turn to the hitherto sleepy river crossing becoming the rail center of central Texas, and hence the place everyone in Texas seemed to pass through sooner or later.

Longarm had been there before, and he'd naturally made note of the location of Madame Lunette's house of ill repute while back in San Antone. It was still a hard row to hoe for a man with a train to catch.

Madame Lunette's lay cheek by jowl with other such establishments and an infamous card house near the river, along a cinder service road between the railroad trestle and toll bridge. That made the disreputable neighborhood handy to rail or toll road traffic while hiding it from respectable folks on higher ground.

The shadows were lengthening, but the afternoon light was still good enough to read by after Longarm had overshot the place, then retraced his steps to see that, sure enough, the numbers over a boarded-up front entrance went with those in his notebook.

There was no call to move up the steps for a tighter look at the small print. The Rangers always posted the same printed notice when they shut a business down, whether for back taxes or one too many back-shootings. They'd already told him what they'd thought of Madame Lunette's disgusting stage shows. They'd likely be able to tell him at the Ranger station whether French Dorothy, the true love of the late Grat Jones, had gone to work anywhere convenient.

He fished out his pocket watch and consulted it as, across the way, a fat lady hung her naked tits over a windowsill to ask if he was lost. He shook his head and put his watch away. Catching a bite to eat before he caught that night train made more sense. For even if they had a dining car attached for the night run north, the price you paid for food on the train these days was a scandal.

Knowing the way back better than he'd known where he'd find the shut-down whorehouse, Longarm cut through an alley, across a weedy vacant lot, and along another back way running behind a cotton gin and some open-sided storage sheds. The stacks of five-hundred-pound bales came in mighty handy when someone behind him shouted, "Longarm! Look out!" and a serious six-gun blazed three times while Longarm made a running dive for cover.

He slid across cotton lint and dust in a narrow slot between two stacks as he got his own .44-40 out. He heard another shot ring out as he rose. It sounded less serious than those first rounds of at least .45-70 lobbed his way by someone seriously intent on inflicting bodily harm.

Longarm edged along the slot, his own less lethal but lethal enough weapon ahead of him. He knew his assailant would have one hell of an edge out in the open with a pistol throwing army rifle rounds. But at anything like reasonable pistol range that other man's freak gun was just going to kick like a mule and maybe throw his aim off just the cat's whisker that could count a heap at such times.

A million silent years passed by. Then someone called out to him, "You still with us, Longarm?"

Longarm started moving back, in hopes of circling in behind the noisy cuss now that he had him located. Then the same voice called out, "It's all right. We got him. Only I've no idea who the son of a bitch might have been!"

Longarm wasn't so sure now. The corrugated tin roofing above all these cotton bales made voices echo a mite. He faced the other way to take advantage of that as he called back, "Was he packing a Remington Rider conversion under a black Spanish hat and who the hell are you?"

The mysterious voice called back, "He was all in black and you had his pistol pegged, Longarm. So who was he? I'd be Morgan Durante of the Pinkerton Agency, by the way. Do I have to tell you why I've taken a personal interest in this shit?"

Longarm called back, half convinced, "Not hardly. I was the one who found that other Pink called Durante up in Denver. I take it you were kin?"

"My brother," the unseen voice called back, adding bitterly, "I've been working the case on my own. I can't afford the agency's rates and they don't track down anyone for free."

Longarm frowned thoughtfully and replied, "I heard different. Old Allan Pinkerton is said to avenge his agents if only as a matter of sound business practice. Might you have been using names such as Marner, Moran, and so on as you dogged my ass the last few days?"

The man calling himself Durante now chuckled dryly and explained, "I told you I was working on my own. The boss may go through some of the motions when we lose an operator. But his sound business practice doesn't extend to risking his state charters with even harmless fibs. So all right, I lie a lot. Are you going to stay holed up forever, or would you like to come out and tell me who I just shot for you?"

Longarm called back, "If there's nobody there but you. You ought to feel safe enough with your own gun holstered and your hands polite as you sort of walk this way."

When Duranted demanded, "Which way is that?" Longarm directed him to move the length of the shed till Longarm spotted him and called out, "Freeze!"

It was the same squat cuss in a rusty black suit who'd played hide-and-go-seek with him around the telegraph office that time. He'd been told to freeze, but he still turned to face Longarm, empty hands at shoulder height, as he called back, "Could we go somewhere else to compare notes? We're likely to have company here any minute."

Longarm moved out to join him, saying, "I'll take it personal if I see you draw for no good reason. They were running in pairs if I'm guessing right about the one you just nailed. Where might that one be?"

Durante pointed back the way he'd come, saying, "The bird on your tail seemed alone. I'd been tailing you more professional from further back. So I was watching him a spell before he threw down on your back. That's his boot sticking out between yonder bales."

Longarm moved closer, peered into the slit in the tricky light, and hunkered down, gun in hand, to grab a booted ankle and haul the face-down cadaver out for a better look.

The Pinkerton man rolled the body on its back with a casual kick. The front of the familiar black sateen shirt was really messy. A soft-nosed .38-30 made a bigger hole coming out than going in. Without that Spanish hat the dead man had wound up bald. Longarm was surprised for as long as it took him to recognize the face as one that had been avoiding his eye in that saloon back in Halfway. The Pinkerton man's voice was pleading as he insisted, "Let's get the hell away from here, damn it. You may want to spend the night in some infernal Ranger station, but this could mean my job! I ain't paid to guard the lives of the great unwashed for *free*!"

Longarm sighed and got out his badge as he replied. "I have a train to catch and my baggage figures to go on to Denver without me if I ain't there within the hour. But you can't just leave dead bodies about like cigar butts, damn it."

He holstered his unfired six-gun and turned toward the distant sounds of a tin whistle, pinning his federal badge to the front of his denim jacket as he muttered, "Let me do the talking and it might not take as long. What'll you bet the rascal you just shot was wanted for shooting folks, somewhere else?"

There was no answer. Longarm took but one more step forward, turned back, and saw that he and the dead man seemed to be alone in the dark shade of the overhead roofing. So he headed back the way he'd just come, hissing softly but firmly, "Come back here, you backshooting asshole! This just ain't *fair*, God damn your eyes!"

He heard distant shouting now. He ducked down an aisle between the bales, quietly calling, "I said I could talk our way clear! I'm a federal lawman assigned to be down this way, and we can say I'd already asked you to back my play."

There was no answer. Longarm tried. He had to try. But there was no way to track a sneak across cement through a maze of burlap-bound baled cotton twelve feet high!

He gave up after he'd circled a spell, and drifted back toward the sound of voices near the place where the man in black had fallen. He was so pissed about missing his train he'd have likely told the copper badges the whole story had they asked him. But before they could ask him Longarm heard one chortle, "Oh, Lordy, we're rich! Don't

131

you know who this one was, Mike?"

Longarm paused in the shadows to hear the local lawman declare, "It's Blacky Bordon from Laredo, just sure as hell! He went bad during the Reconstruction, shooting niggers gratis till they had federal warrants out on him and he turned full-time professional."

Longarm might have heard more, had he hung around. But there was still a chance he might catch that train if he ran like hell, and a night spent getting somewhere had rehashing the same story beat. So he slipped away, circled, and made for the depot as fast as a man could move without attracting undue attention.

He had to keep an eye peeled for that sneaky Pink, and the younger and shabbier gunslick who'd been traveling with Blacky Bordon too, as he cut through many an alley in the fading light.

Chapter 14

It hadn't been easy. The last few yards had involved some serious running along a railroad platform and a mad grab for the rear rails of a receding observation platform. But as darkness fell Longarm had recovered his breath with a beer and a smoke in a corner chair of the club car.

He'd chosen that particular position lest anyone try to sneak up behind him. So he got to watch Morgan Durante, with some distaste, as the older Pink ordered his own schooner of beer at the bar and then drift back to join him, smiling innocently.

Durante didn't *sound* sarcastic as he asked if the seat next to Longarm's was taken. But Longarm let his own venom drip as he growled, "Thanks for holding the train for me. I know why them other birds have been following me. I'm still waiting to hear why you were."

Durante sat down, sipped some suds, and calmly replied, "You seem to be where all the action is. As you know, my agency was retained by Miss Kate Thayer after she'd received those crank letters. My brother was but one of the Pinkerton agents assigned to watch over her. So it was the luck of the draw, nothing personal, when he was murdered."

Durante took another thoughtful sip before he added ominously, "Murdered after you'd moved him from watching the girl to watching Senator Fraser. Our Denver supervisor wasn't happy about that, by the way. Neither you nor the senator had retained us!"

Longarm made a wry face and muttered, "Tough shit. Nobody had ever threatened the Thayer gal. The letters she got only said her family lawyer and trustee was a war criminal. I'm sorry as hell about your brother. But doesn't his death prove the real target was old Senator Fraser?"

Durante flatly answered, "No. Nobody had made any attempt to back up those written threats with live action before my brother was killed guarding against them. And nothing has happened to the senator since, which is even odder. It's like I told you. All the serious action seems to take place around *you*, and you alone! Not the Thayer girl, not the senator, his staff, his kith and kin, or . . . what do you need, a diagram on the blackboard?"

Longarm stared down into his half-empty beer schooner for a spell before he reluctantly replied, "You're on to something. I said in the beginning that nine out of ten threatening letters add up to no more'n a cowardly enemy making empty threats. Those letters in particular add up to false accusations as well, unless the letter writer knows something neither the Union nor the Confederacy ever recorded."

Durante said, "I know. I visited the same historical societies."

Longarm said, "I talked to blood kin of at least one of Fraser's so-called victims too. Trooper Masters couldn't have been executed by anyone in Chivington's command. That Corporal Alcott, said to have led the lost patrol, was never assigned to Pyron's rebel column, which was the one Chivington's famous Four Hundred tangled with. So how do you like some personal or political enemy just making up a lot of spiteful bull to cast doubt on the senator's military record?"

Durante said, "I'd like it better if my brother hadn't been stabbed in the back carrying out your orders. You're the one they seem out to finish off. What sort of mail have *you* been getting lately?"

Longarm set the rest of his beer aside and gripped his cheroot more firmly between his bared teeth as he answered honestly, "Not one line. I follow your drift. What if, all this time, some personal enemy has been after me and me alone? What if them loco letters were only designed to . . . That's where I get stuck. Marshal Vail might have assigned another deputy to the case, and then where would the letter writer have been?"

Durante pointed out, "No worse off than before. My agency tried in vain to trace those letters to Kate Thayer back to their sender. You know how much luck you've had, following directions to West Texas. Anyone who knew you well enough to really hate you would figure Billy Vail would send his senior deputy. If Vail had sent some other hand, your secret admirer could have simply pulled in his horns. But Vail *did* send you, you *did* follow those written hints to leave Denver alone, and aren't you glad I was interested in you too when that cuss got the drop on you back there?"

Longarm swallowed the sudden dry taste in his mouth and sipped a little beer to wash it down before he muttered, "I was too sore at you to say thanks. But consider it said, and I reckon it's just as well we're on our way back to Denver. I see what you mean about some secret pal wanting me alone in unfamiliar surroundings. Old Billy Vail and my other pals would be more likely to solve my murder in Denver if the mastermind behind all this shit hails from there as well!"

Durante nodded soberly and said, "I'd like them to solve another murder while they were at it. It was my idea for my brother and me to go to work for the Pinks after the War Department cut back on Indian scouting. So I feel sort of responsible for poor Dave."

He sipped some more, then softly added, "I told you I've been out tracking on my own. I'm going to have to put in more time trailing errant wives if I want to keep my job. But we ought to be able to stay in touch and . . . Who do you think we're after?"

Longarm shrugged. "If I knew, I'd say so. Right now, your guess is as good as mine. But unless the rascal sends more mail, I reckon I'll ignore that distraction for now."

Durante asked, "You mean you agree those letters were designed to throw you off?"

To which Longarm could only reply, "They *did*, didn't they? As you just said yourself, nobody's made any real moves against the senator or anyone close to him, while meanwhile I've been getting shot at regular, proving there doesn't seem to be a lick of truth or even common sense to those fool letters!"

He took an annoyed drag on his cheroot and let the smoke shoot out his nostrils before he added, "I mean to buckle down and go back over death threats made against me personally in the eight or ten years I've been packing a badge for Uncle Sam!"

The sardonic older man reached inside his frock coat as he sighed and said, "I wish you hadn't said that. I want the son of a bitch who killed my brother, and the professional courtesy I just extended back there amid those cotton bales may or may not have done the deed. Meanwhile I'm running out of time and you must think you're slick as hell."

He handed Longarm his opened billfold as he added, "What were you aiming to do, wire my agency from some watering stop along the way?"

Longarm smiled sheepishly as he studied the Pinkerton papers and fancy private badge. As if to confirm the promise of the staring open eye and the motto "We Never Sleep!" the man who'd handed the badge to him said, "I work out of the Cheyenne branch. My supervisor is Senior Agent Joseph Shannon. He'll deny sending me to Texas or even as far south as Denver. That's because he gave me leave to attend my brother's funeral back East. The agency arranged to have the body shipped home."

Longarm handed the billfold back, saying, "I heard the Pinks took care of their own. So how come you have to look into your brother's murder on the sneak? Don't your main office care about an agent being stabbed in the back on duty?"

Durante put the billfold away as he morosely replied, "He wasn't killed on duty for the agency. He'd been assigned to guard Miss Kate Thayer, not the gallery of the Colorado State Senate. So Allan Pinkerton, being a Scotchman, feels he's being big enough about funeral expenses. He's not about to spring for a full-scale investigation of a private killing. Pinkerton men who get killed in whorehouses on their own time are on their own as well."

"Unless they have close kin," said Longarm soberly.

Durante shrugged. "Close kin with their own fish to fry and their own jobs to worry about. I was planning on spending another few days in your pleasant company in hopes you'd flush the rascals for me. Maybe you have. Any of the hired guns we've taken out between us so far could have been the one who killed old Dave."

Longarm asked, "Don't you want to know who might have ordered it and why?"

To which the more worldly older man replied with a wistful little smile, "I'd like to know a heap of things I'll never know, starting with how high is up and how long is forever. But if I don't get back to Cheyenne within the week, there's likely to be a real mystery about my room and board. I ain't pretty enough to live off my landlady on her lust for me alone, and like you just said, we could be talking about some grudge left over from a case you worked on years ago!"

Chapter 15

Counting that tedious layover in Wichita, the dogleg trip up to Denver figured to take around eighteen hours. So Longarm wrangled a Pullman compartment from a conductor he'd ridden with before, and figuring he didn't want to sleep with Morgan Durante or vice versa, turned in alone around nine to get started on the written report old Billy Vail was sure to demand in justification for all the time he'd spent down Texas way.

By breakfast time he'd lost track of the Pinkerton man. He didn't care. He'd wired Durante's Cheyenne office during that water stop at the Red River, and found their answer waiting at the Wichita Western Union when he got off to grub up and wait for the westbound he had to switch to. Cheyenne confirmed they did indeed have an agent named Morgan Durante who stood about five feet nine, weighed just under two hundred pounds with graying sandy hair, and had surely taken time off to attend his brother's funeral down by Little Rock.

That explained why Durante didn't seem anxious to board the train to Denver with him, Arkansas being the other direction entirely, so the already travel-weary deputy took his time with the extra coffee, made a careful selection of magazines out at the tobacco stand, and still wound up bored and fidgety by the time he finally rolled into Denver after an eternity spent staring out at the rolling sea of shortgrass called the High Plains or Great American Desert, depending on whether you were raising cows or trying to get somewhere.

The workday was better than half shot by the time Longarm had hauled his saddle and possibles home and changed into clean linens and the sissy three-piece tweed suit they expected him to wear over to the Federal Building. But he figured it was safer to report in just long enough to quit for the day than it might be to fib about railroad timetables to an old paper-trailer like Billy Vail.

He was right. Before he could sit down and light up in the back office, the crusty Vail growled, "Have Henry type your scrawls up so's my old eyes can make some sense of it. Then get your lazy ass up to the Fraser place on the double. Miss Elsbeth just sent word by a house servant that someone just sent her brother, the senator, one of them love letters."

Longarm nodded and said he was on his way. Before he could leave his boss added, "Watch your back along the way. It's my understanding the letter wound up in their letter box without no stamp."

Longarm cocked a thoughtful eyebrow and observed, "Meaning it was hand-delivered, by the writer or somebody who has to know who wrote it?"

Vail snorted, "I just said that. It gets spookier when you consider Denver P.D. has been replaced by a round-the-clock guard detail of state troopers!"

To which Longarm could only reply with a thin smile, "I'd feel a mite safer guarded by full-time lawmen instead of part-time troopers."

Vail shrugged and said, "Governor's orders, and mayhaps he knows what he's doing. Denver could only spare a couple of copper badges at a time. The governor's ordered a full guard mount, a squad at a time, standing two hours on and four hours off with the corporal of the guard and

139

supernumeraries posted in the house. The Fraser place has spacious servant quarters."

Longarm said he'd make sure of that, and left. Since he was still on the department's time he hailed a hansom cab out front, and got up to the senator's big brownstone a lot faster than he could have legged it. He didn't get sore when a part-time soldier blue barred his way up the front steps with a bayonetted Springfield held at port and made him show some damned identification. But as the kid allowed he'd been recognized and might as well go on in, Longarm pointed with his chin at the mail slot of the big front door and asked, "How do you reckon somebody put a letter through there without being challenged, old son?"

The guardsman sounded sure of himself as he replied, "Not through *this* child, Deputy Long. Rain or shine, night or day, I walks my post in a military manner, keeping always on the alert—"

"And reporting anything unusual on or about my post to the corporal of the guard," Longarm finished, having had to memorize the same general orders in his own time. The seventh general order forbade anyone pulling guard detail to engage in long-winded conversations with anyone, so Longarm mentioned the "silent seventh" and moved on.

The front door swung open before he got to knock. It was one of their prissy hall porters in a boiled shirt and cutaway coat. Longarm managed not to grin as the jasper took his hat and allowed the madame would receive him in the study.

Old Elsbeth Fraser looked more manly as she rose from her perch near a mahogany secretary to hold out an envelope. As he took it from her Longarm saw it was simply addressed to "Killer Fraser," with no other indication where it had been meant to go. Billy Vail had already said there'd be no stamp or postmark.

As he opened the envelope he told the worried-looking older woman, "We've had no luck with the stationary, ma'am. It's a cheap mock-bond you can buy in many a neighborhood notions shop. It's sold by the box and it's doubtful the clerk who sold it to your brother's tormentor would remember selling a dime purchase to anyone who only had one head. Has the senator seen this one by the way?"

The senator's spinster sister pursed her lips primly and said, "He hasn't come home yet. I naturally sent word to his office as soon as I found that abomination in our afternoon mail, but—"

"What time was that, ma'am?" he asked. "It's important, seeing I just got challenged on your steps and they relieve out front every other hour, likely on the hour."

She sighed and said, "The officer in charge already asked me that. I fear I wasn't much help to him either. I'd been doing some needlework after dining alone in my quarters a little after noon. I came downstairs around two-thirty or three. I asked our butler, Beverly, whether the afternoon mail had arrived. He told me there hadn't been any in the box when last he'd looked. But naturally he went out in the hall to the door to look again. That latest letter you're holding is all he found."

By this time Longarm had scanned the short message, which demanded the senator confess on the senate floor to his crimes or be shot down like the dog he was.

Longarm told the worried-looking spinster, "I just got back from Texas and comparing notes with some kith and kin of the rebels your brother's accused of murdering, ma'am. If it's any comfort, nobody I met down yonder thinks your brother done it. Union records fail to put him in the right times or places, and better yet, Confederate records back him up. More than one rebel raider these fool letters say he murdered in cold blood seem to have wound up dead on another part of the battlefield entirely. I'd best hold on to this anyway."

When she said she wanted to show it to her brother Longarm replied, "I can show it to him just as easy, ma'am. Meanwhile I want to see if I can match it up with other handwriting. I don't mean other death threats sent unsigned. I mean signed documents written by the same hand in a more innocent manner."

She didn't seem to understand. He explained. "We can assume these nasty letters were sent by somebody with a grudge against an elected official who doubtless deals with many a complaint or request from a heap of constituents. So what if we were to find an irate but *signed* letter demanding a state senator do something about water rights, mineral rights, or some foolishness about paying taxes on land their family never paid the Indians for in the first place?"

She dimpled in sudden understanding, hardly a tempting sight, told Longarm he was ever so smart, and then threw her big old arms around him for what he hoped was meant as a sisterly hugging and kissing.

She didn't kiss bad for such a dignified-looking old gal, and it was tough to keep from responding in kind when a lady ground her old ring-dang-do against the front of your pants like that. But Longarm had met up with antique spinster gals before, and no matter how flirty one might behave in her innocent ignorance, he knew they tended to climb right up the drapes, bleating like lost lambs, if a man really made a play for them.

So he got loose as best he could, without hitting a lady, and lit out for the Capitol Building without asking whether the senator would still be there.

As he strode north along the sandstone walk, it seemed he was not alone in his confusion about the private lives being led in or about the Fraser place. He slowed down when he heard boot heels overtaking him, and found himself strolling through the late afternoon light under the cottonwoods atop Capitol Hill with a portly cuss who looked like a bank teller and likely was, most of the time. But at the moment he was wearing army blue and sporting two gold stripes on either sleeve. The Roman numerals on his choke collar put him in the Second Colorado Cav. Billy Vail had said the corporal of their guard was on the Fraser premises.

Longarm nodded and said, "Evening. I'm sorry I lit out without a courtesy call, Corporal. But I'm anxious to catch up with Senator Fraser before he leaves his office for the day, if he ain't already."

The noncom said, "Listen, there's no way in hell some kid could have slipped that letter through the front door into the letter box with one of my men posted smack by the front steps!"

Longarm replied, "Never said it was a kid. But that would make it a tad easier. Say you're relieving the ten-to-twelve guard at noon. So the three of you are down at the foot of the steps whilst some spry street urchin rolls over a porch rail down to one end and—"

"Say that sissy butler, Beverly, checked that mail box around one," the corporal put in. "Meaning Trooper Culhane, a good man, was on the damned porch or no farther than the front walk, wide awake in broad-ass daylight when your invisible delivery boy poked that letter through the mail slot, which has a brass flap inclined to clang, by the way!"

Longarm shrugged and said, "A man can cock a gun as noisy or as quiet as he has a mind to. I wasn't there. So I can't say how it was done. But somebody done it. I have the letter in my coat pocket as we speak. Now I'm fixing to compare the handwriting with regular mail delivered less mysteriously to the senator's office."

The corporal suggested, "Has anybody examined the handwriting of those mysterious sissy servant boys back there to the house? I'll bet you didn't know that butler, called *Beverly* for Gawd's sake, has been taking it up the ass from the other sissy boys and not a single woman working there!"

Longarm made a wry face and said, "Rich folks are like that. Single female servants can cause more trouble on the back stairs than a sissy boy nobody in the family would be interested in and vice versa. They say Queen Victoria has a whole crew of sissy boys at Buckingham Palace, and going by the tales they tell about the Prince of Wales, it's small wonder. Otherwise they'd have a hell of a time getting their tea served with His Royal Horniness pinching bottoms. The Turks have far more drastic ways of keeping their household help in line. But they'd never stand for even Queen Victoria cutting her butler's balls off."

The corporal confided he doubted any man named Beverly could have balls to begin with.

Longarm shrugged and said, "I ain't interested in him that way. If it's any comfort my boss, Marshal Vail, had some expert look at the handwriting of everyone working for the senator. That's how come I'm off to compare this latest letter with other samples. But seeing I got an expert on the Colorado Guard to consult, am I correct when I assume the Colorado Volunteers, like other state militia units, were federalized during the war?"

The member of the Colorado Guards said, "During and right after, in a series of actions by Congress. As you doubtless know, traitor governors called out their Southern state militias to create their Confederate Army overnight, right after Fort Sumter was fired upon by the South Carolina Militia on orders of their governor. As I well recall, there was a heap of confusion early on as state militias in states like Tennessee made up their mind which side they were on. So once it got sorted out, Washington made sure such bull would be a mite less likely by changing the rules."

He was telling Longarm things he already knew. So Longarm said, "Right. The former state militias were declared one national guard with the state and federal governments sharing authority."

The corporal continued relentlessly. "Meaning the local governor can still call out his state guards during a local

144

emergency, but the federal War Department has the final say and gets to call us up for a *national* emergency, such as another war with Canada."

Longarm said soothingly, "The last one was a draw. I doubt either side wants another, despite all that Yankee-baiting during their last election up yonder. The point I'm more interested in involves wartime records. The modern guard would have the original handwritten militia records on hand somewhere, right?"

The guardsman said he didn't know. Longarm thanked him anyway and they parted friendly.

Others were coming south from the municipal buildings and business district of Denver by the time he reached the State House. He went on in anyway, in hopes the senator kept more fashionable supper hours.

He saw how close he'd timed it when he met the senator and the spectacular Widow Dunbar in the rotunda. As they shook hands the senator said he and his true love were bound for that fancy French place on Welton Street. Longarm envied the older man for more than the fancy grub he got to eat. Getting kissed French by an older woman wouldn't hurt at all if she was built like Fionna Dunbar!

Longarm showed the senator the letter and explained his reasons for toting it all the way over there. The senator said his secretary might still be there to let him in, and gave Longarm carte blanche to go through all the papers he might find in the suite of offices. So Longarm took the letter back and legged it down the crowded corridor to catch that pretty gal with the sour expression in the act of locking up for the night.

The news that he had the senator's permission to go through their files didn't sweeten her expression worth mentioning. She had her straw summer hat pinned atop her upswept mouse-colored hair in a no-nonsense way that warned him she was in a hurry to get to her own supper. So he told her he could lock up later.

She sniffed and said, "No, you can't. It locks from the outside with a key and I don't have a spare key for you. But orders are orders and I want you to catch that person too. So let's just *do* it."

They went back inside and got right to it. She sat him at her own desk and commenced to bring him file drawers of letters in manila folders. Longarm noted with approval she or someone who knew their business had filed different letters from different constituents according to topic. He agreed with her when she suggested they might save time by just looking at gripes. Voters writing in to express a great admiration for their state senator seemed less likely to write him death threats on separate sheets of paper.

Her name turned out to be Una Gordon. That hardly seemed worth such a surly view of the world. When he asked her if her name, like that of her employer, might not be Scotch, she snapped, "Scottish, if you don't mind. As a matter of fact Miss Elsbeth Fraser mentioned my clan favorably when she interviewed me for the job. I'd almost forgotten my grandparents came from Scotland before my father had been born."

He said he'd thought her name sounded clannish, and kept poking through a folder of gripes about mining claims. It wouldn't have been kind to say he suspected he knew why the handsome senator's bossy sister had chosen another born spinster from among the other applicants. It made a cruel sort of sense, like having an upstairs maid who shaved every other day at least. So how might one ask a drab employee how often her boss got in trouble over better-looking gals? None of the pissing and moaning about mineral rights seemed written in the same hand as the death threat he'd spread on the desk blotter to match them up with.

As Una came in with yet another load—this one bitching about water rights, she said—he smiled up at her and said, "This figures to take us a spell and it's already past my usual suppertime, Miss Una. Would it

146

get you in Dutch with your regular swain if I was to take you to supper just over on Colfax so we could finish this tedious chore less famished later?"

She started to say something, caught herself, and asked incredulously, "You're asking me to go *out* with you, Deputy Long?"

He said, "Just to supper, ma'am. It's safe to call me Custis. I seldom propose anything, decent or otherwise, at the supper table."

She laughed, a vast improvement, and allowed she was half starved. So seeing she'd never taken off her dumb little hat, Longarm put his Stetson back on and took her to that same place near the cathedral, just across the avenue.

He'd suggested it for the same reasons he'd suggested it before. The place was fancy enough for a lady but simple enough for him to afford. But from the way Una acted as they were led to their table, one might have thought she didn't get taken to supper all that often. When their waiter asked Longarm if he and the lady would care for something to drink before they looked at the menu, the poor little drab looked so confused that Longarm ordered them both sissy rum juleps instead of the boilermaker he'd had in mind for himself. When Una protested she didn't drink, he assured her he'd figured as much and said, "That's how come I ordered what I did, ma'am. A rum punch is a tall thin drink you can nurse clean through a party without getting drunk or looking like a spoilsport. I can't vouch for the liver and onions on their menu, and they make their chili con carne too mild. Everything else I've ever ordered here turned out tolerable, though."

She decided on sliced steak. He knew she'd think he was showing off if he suggested she order something more expensive. So he allowed he liked sliced steak too, and asked if she wanted a salad or soup first.

He admired her thrifty nature even more when she said she'd go for the black bean soup. Paying these prices for glorified water was bad enough. But at least she didn't order rabbit food sold for the price of human.

When they got their drinks first, Una sipped, gasped, and whispered, "Are you sure there's no liquor in this, Custis?"

He confided, "Just enough rum to give it some flavor. It's mostly fruit punch and shaved ice."

So she said that in that case she'd drink it, and did so fast enough to need two more before coffee and dessert. But Longarm hadn't lied all that much about the alcoholic content, and so the only effect that much rum had on her was an improvement in her poor little face. He'd been right about her being almost pretty, save for that sour expression she usually wore. Once a good warm meal and a little rum had relaxed her a mite, Longarm felt less silly about being seen in public with her. So he asked if she'd like a second slice of cheese cake to go with a second cup of coffee.

She took that as a kid might after finding the tooth fairy had left a whole four bits under her pillow. Then, to cover up, she had to scowl at him some more and say, "Well, seeing we may have to stay awake quite a while."

Longarm asked their waiter to make sure their coffee was strong enough to strip the silver plate off their spoons. Then he told her she reminded him of a Scotch joke.

She protested, "It's not true we're stingy, Custis. It was a poor country and the people had to be thrifty, is all."

He said, "I'm not fixing to tell the one about Wee Angus. I had one in mind about this old Scotchman who goes to his doctor about this bad cough. You heard it?"

She was blushing and unable to meet his eye as she murmured, "No. But I think I heard the one about Wee Angus."

He said, "This one's clean. The doc tells MacTavish he needs more fresh air after working in the mill all week. So he orders him to go fishing over on the loch every Sunday till his lungs clear up. But the first Sunday he's fishing by the loch, who should come along but Deacon MacDugal from his own Calvinist kirk."

Una said, "Ooh! Fishing on the Sabbath?"

Longarm nodded soberly and said, "That's what the deacon thought. But as soon as MacTavish explains, the deacon considers, decides it's all right as long as it's to save his health, providing and *only* providing MacTavish doesn't *enjoy* himself."

She looked blank. Longarm repeated the last line, sighed, and said, "The Jacobite Catholic Scot who told me that one said no Calvinist would get it. You're still a heap prettier when you smile, Miss Una. Ain't you allowed to like *anything*?"

She sat up straighter and demurely replied, "I liked those rum drinks just fine. Have you been trying to get me drunk and have your wicked way with me, good sir?"

He laughed incredulously and replied, "I don't turn water into wine nor cast out evil spirits either, ma'am!" Then he saw the hurt in her gray eyes and gallantly added, "I mean anyone can see you ain't that kind of a lassie, ma'am."

Then, to change the subject, he asked, "Could we get something else straight, Miss Una? I've noticed most of the state senators have offices over to the Senate Building across the Capitol grounds. So how might a particular senator rate his own layout smack inside the State House with the governor and other state officials?"

As the waiter brought their second servings of coffee and dessert, she explained how Senator Fraser *was* a state official in addition to standing up for his county in the senate. As they washed down cake with coffee, she explained that Fraser chaired more than one committee and sat on the governor's mining and irrigation boards—which meant, as Longarm saw better than she did, a big frog in position to make a lot of enemies in his one little puddle.

Walking her back to the State House he mused, as much to himself as to her, "I figured that wild-goose chase I was on down Texas way was unjustified by anything Senator Fraser could have done back in his misspent youth as a part-time trooper. It does seem to me a comrade-in-arms with a grudge left over from the war could come up with far better charges. I mean, if I was out to defame some old boy I served with at, say, Shiloh, I'd never give him the wrong job with the wrong rank. Come to study on it, I don't know *how* I'd ever manage to name specific enemy troopers he'd done anything to. I mean, unless we captured an enemy trooper, we seldom had a chance to ask his name and address. Yet Confederate records show some of those old boys the senator's supposed to have murdered were never captured at all!"

The hall inside was dark as well as deserted, once Una let them in with her key to the side entrance. As they moved along the sort of spooky corridor she took his arm with a little shudder, saying, "Senator Fraser's already pointed that out, Custis. He had me send for a list of all the rebels captured or even identified for burial during that one campaign he took part in. Not one of those reb scouts mentioned in those letters was ever captured by anyone in the senator's regiment! He thinks it's all over his fight against free silver. Some foolish granger who thinks he can wipe out all his debts with inflated silver certificates must be trying to scare the senator into hiding. It's the only motive that makes any sense."

As she let him into the office he nodded, but pointed out, "It does reduce outstanding debts when you inflate the money supply before you have to pay off. Say you borrowed a thousand dollars when President Hayes had dollars pegged at twenty to the ounce of gold. Then say you drove the price of silver way down, so you could pay off in silver certificates worth less'n half what they'd be worth if the price of silver stayed tied in with gold."

"We *know* how inflation robs Peter to pay Paul," Una declared. "That's why the senator's against free silver to the last breath. I'll see what we have on constituents who may have granger leanings, no matter what they've written in about."

He said he was impressed by her cross-index filing, but he wanted to see more personal stuff.

When she asked what he meant he explained, "There's thousands of letters from the general public and even if we had the time, I've had time to brood on how *personal* those death threats have been. I mean, how many stockmen or mining men up the other side of the Divide would know their senator had ridden in the war with the Colorado Firsters?"

She said, "A lot of them. Most of our western counties were settled by Union folks, and it never hurts to remind them come election time. I typed up our summation of the senator's war record myself. It wasn't his idea. He's very modest about what he calls his short stint at soldiering. It was the party leader's idea to play up his riding with Chivington's Four Hundred when the opposition put a Quaker and Indian lover against us. We never decided whether it was the senator's fighting for Colorado or the other candidate's mad desire to make peace at any price with the Mountain Utes, but . . ."

"I follow your drift," Longarm said, rising from her desk as he insisted, "I'd still like to poke through any personal letters he might have left about, Miss Una. I doubt any Mountain Ute is trying to scare him at this late date. Most all in his part of the state wound up on their way across the Green River whether any white folks stood up for 'em or not. I know, because I tried standing up for some and look where it got us."

Then he headed for the senator's inner office. "I know nobody from the Fraser household writes the letter R a certain way. I'd sure like to know if someone else the senator gets personal mail from, like that party leader, writes that way when he or she ain't trying to disguise their handwriting."

She nodded and let him in with yet another key, murmuring, "I'm going to have to tell him you were back here."

Longarm said that sounded fair as he struck a match to light a wall fixture. He lit the senator's desk lamp as well, sat down, and started opening drawers while little Una commenced to look sour some more. He noticed the senator's Navy Colt was missing. He was just as glad. At least the older man was taking the threats *that* seriously.

There weren't that many personal letters. Una said she'd filed the ones that needed serious attention. He found a note from Kate Thayer. The senator had likely failed to feel she really needed more money. The infernal letter, a complaining one, was mostly typed on her own infernal Remington-Sholes. So the only handwritten R was the last one of her last name. It looked more like a butte on the skyline than a bobwire sticker or tight V. The other letters looked nothing like the handwritten death threat in his other hand either. But that got him to ask the more professional typist, "Wouldn't it make a lot more sense to type up death threats and not sign 'em at all than it would to send unsigned messages in disguised handwriting?"

She asked how he knew the death threat handwriting was disguised. He said, "Every word is spaced and slanted the same careful way in a sort of schoolbook Spencerian script, save for that one old-timey R Professor P.R. Spencer might not have gone along with."

Una moved over closer, asking what he was talking about. When he showed her she said, "That's the way a lot of folks from Europe make that one letter. Folks west of New York City tend to use the style you call modern. Either can be correct."

To which he could only reply, "Not in *my* little schoolhouse back in West-by-God-Virginia. But bless your better education anyway. Who do we have from Europe to suspect, Miss Una?"

She thought before she decided, "There must be dozens among the political friends and foes of poor Senator Fraser. The only *close* friend that comes to mind won't work as an enemy, though."

He asked who they were talking about and why he or she wouldn't work, adding, "You'd be surprised who can hate a man if they only put their mind to it."

Una shook her head and insisted, "The Widow Dunbar was born in the Lowlands and proud of it, to hear her brag about some old castle. But she'd hardly work as an enemy! I mean, I walked in on them one evening in this very office and, well, you did mention that silly joke about Wee Angus!"

Then she blushed and turned away as Longarm asked, in a broad Scots brogue, "You mean the one where they asked Wee Angus what he wanted for his birthday, an' he said he wanted a watch, an' say they *let* him?"

She laughed despite herself and blurted out, "Right on that desk, with her on top, the brazen thing!"

He shrugged and said, "Well, mayhaps she was worried about what her household help would say. I can guess what his big sister would say. But I follow your drift about her sending him death threats in between times."

He rummaged some more, and came up with another letter from the less adoring Kate Thayer. She'd typed this one as well, but added a postscript about some bills in her own handwriting. Longarm went over her neat but less Spencerian script a letter at a time before deciding aloud, "Nobody disguising their handwriting that much would have call to change their natural R's and I dots as well."

Una shifted her weight nervously and asked, "Is this going to take much longer, Custis? The landlady where I board is very strict and has a vicious mind. I dasn't repeat the things she accused me of the time I supped with another secretary and lost track of the time!"

Longarm didn't ask the gender of the other secretary. He dug out another perfumed note from the Widow Dunbar

153

and said, "Look how she dots her I's with bitty circles. Then compare that, along with her funny way of writing the letter R, with these nastier notes on cheaper paper. The sneak writing the threatening letters *tries* to avoid circular dots over the letter I, but slips up every now and again."

He carefully folded a particularly mushy note from the senator's true love and tucked it away in a pocket as Una gasped, "You can't take anything from the senator's desk, Custis!"

To which he could only reply, "Sure I can. I just did. I'll tell him I took it, and why, should he ever miss it. Meanwhile I want a handwriting expert to look at it more scientifically for us. I swear I'll be confounded if it turns out Miss Fionna has been writing alternate love letters and death threats to her true love. But if I live to be a hundred I'll just never understand women, so there you are."

Una suddenly gasped, "Dear Lord! They've come back!" and moved over to blow out the wall sconce as Longarm shut the drawer, then said, "That's all right. The senator gave me permission to work late in his office. Reckon he didn't think I'd be working quite this late. But when you're caught you're caught, so . . ."

Then she'd blown out the desk lamp and taken him by the hand to lead him the wrong way, it seemed to him, as they both heard jolly laughter out front.

Then they were somehow on a dimly lit but visible flight of marble stairs, and Una was locking the door they'd just slipped out through. Longarm gazed about, trying to get his bearings as the gal whispered, "All lawyers have side exits to their office suites and these were built with lawyers in mind."

He said, "Must come in handy when you're handling both sides in a sticky family matter and, right, we're on the steps leading up to the dome above the rotunda."

She started to tug on him some more, whispering, "Not too loud. We want to go down the other way so we can slip out the far exit."

But he insisted, "Not so fast. I want to be certain that's the senator and his true love. I ain't supposed to run away from jolly burglars, ma'am."

Una hissed, "Are you crazy? Didn't you hear them laughing and carrying on as if they'd had more rum juleps that you and me with their own suppers?"

He whispered back, "Burglars get drunk too. Sometimes a crook who knows an office is empty but a night watchman might be on the premises just acts as if he owns the place to account for the noise and lighting he can't avoid. So hush and let's make sure."

They did. The side door's panels were more economical than the thicker ones on the more impressive front entrance. So they didn't have a lick of trouble making out the Widow Dunbar's words as she trilled, "Make sure you lock that door this time, Jay-Jay. Remember what happened that time your poor secretary caught us in the act."

Longarm didn't look at Una, but he could picture her expression as they both heard the older man laugh indulgently and reply, "It probably did her some good. The poor little mud hen was raised to feel fucking your bridegroom with the lights on was a sure ticket to hellfire and damnation!"

This time it was Longarm who led the way, not saying anything as he hauled the silent Una down a few steps, across the rotunda in the dark, and out the south side entrance of the State House.

It was well after sundown and the stars were winking at them above the blacker outline of the Front Range to the west as, down the grassy slope where lamp-lit Broadway crossed the capitol grounds, some young folks out on the town had stopped to buy hot tamales off the old Mex whose cart was a familiar sight there, weather permitting.

Longarm doubted Una wanted a hot tamale. He said, "Well, I thank you for your help and I'll let you know

155

what our handwriting expert has to say. You want me to walk you home or do we need us a carriage?"

She sobbed, "I'm not a mud hen! I'm not! And I guess I've got my own little secrets that those silly old things would never guess at in a million years!"

He said soothingly, "I think it's silly to sneak into an office like a kid, and with a grown widow woman too. I never said you reminded me of a mud hen, or even a partridge, Miss Una. I'm sure the old cuss was low-rating you to make his old widow woman feel young and pretty. Older gals always suspect younger gals of flirting with all the men they'd rather flirt with their ownselves."

She said, "That's silly. Senator Fraser's old enough to be my father, and he's never tried to get *me* atop his desk that way!"

Longarm chuckled at the picture and said, "He'd be mighty dumb to fool with any of his help, or even a client as pretty as Kate Thayer."

"Do you think that spoiled rich girl is prettier than me?" asked the far plainer secretary in a venomous tone.

It would have been cruel to laugh. So he soberly repeated his question about their intended destination.

Una sighed and said, "My boardinghouse is only a short walk, down on Lincoln Street, this side of that big stone schoolhouse. But what am I ever going to tell my landlady? The old witch refuses to let us have our own keys to the front door and she locks up every night at nine!"

Longarm blinked and reached for his pocket watch as he murmured, "Lord have mercy, I did take up a heap of your time, and it's small wonder the senator thought it was safe to come back for some late work at the office as well!"

Una murmured, "I wish my best friend, Molly, hadn't gone East to get married. Sometimes I used to stay overnight at her place. That way my landlady assumed I'd simply skipped breakfast and gone off to work early. She unlocks her infernal door at dawn."

Longarm said, "Well, I got a suspicious landlady as well. But how do you feel about checking into the Tremont Hotel just for tonight? That way you can freshen up in the morning, enjoy a fine breakfast, and still get back up this hill ahead of your boss."

She gasped, "Why, Custis, whatever gave you such ideas about me? Just because I confided I might not be the goody-goody some take me for hardly means I'm accustomed to checking into hotels with men on such short notice!"

He started to assure her she had him all wrong. But by then he could see, despite the faint light from a nearby street lamp, they had plenty of time to get her on home by her nine o'clock deadline. So he pocketed his watch and only said, "I never invite a real lady to spend the night with me after one supper either, as a general rule. But you have to admit this has been an unusual evening, and it ain't as if either of us *planned* on being forced to be . . . practical?"

She hesitated, then took his arm and gave it a conspiring hug as she murmured, looking the other way, "Well, as long as you promise never to tell a soul and we can stop at a drugstore first."

He did, and they did, and he was afraid, while she was talking mighty softly to a drugstore gal in the back, he was going to have to take a shower back in a damned old India rubber slicker.

But once he'd had a quiet talk with a room clerk he knew of old and they got upstairs at last, the gal her boss described as a mud hen had him flat on his back across the bed with his naked shaft up her wild wet innards before he could get his frock coat or gun rig off. So that's how he knew, once she'd slipped out of her duds and into the adjoining bath with a coy promise to be right back, she was one of those swell pals who knew how to take care of herself afterwards.

Senator Fraser had been wrong about old Una and lamp-lit lovemaking. It was her idea to light a wall fixture and adjust the mirror above the hotel dresser so they could watch themselves going at it dog-style. For in addition to her now-pretty face, her flawless naked body was spectacular and she knew it.

In the end, with Una liking to take it in both ends, he learned she'd adopted that sour expression and those drab duds in hopes of avoiding just this sort of "trouble," as she defined an appetite he found healthy as hell.

When they weren't coming or trying to figure another way to do so, Una liked to cuddle, smoke, and share secrets. But while some of her own were sort of startling, Longarm was unable to learn anything new about the senator's troubles from her. Longarm had already figured the Widow Dunbar liked to drink and screw. Una didn't know who else the senator might have been fooling with on the side. She didn't think the senator had been getting any from Kate Thayer, and Longarm was inclined to agree. Those letters from the younger ward to the horny old cuss hadn't read like those of a young gal asking her older lover for more presents, and the only handwriting that matched up at all didn't make a lick of sense.

Una agreed, toying with the hairs on his bare belly as he mused aloud about gals screwing elderly gents atop a desk and then going home to write death threats.

Una said, "She's still attractive, even without her own handsome income, and the poor besotted senator is so crazy about her he'd do most anything she asked. So why would she have to threaten him to make him do . . . what?"

"Good question," said Longarm, blowing a thoughtful smoke ring as he decided, "If we knew what those threats are meant to inspire the senator to *do,* we'd have a better handle on who's *sending* them."

Then he began to play with her down yonder as he sighed and said, "The senator can't seem to come up with an educated guess. I want to go over all the senator's business you know about for me, as a lawyer and investor as well as a politico, honey."

She demurely asked, "Can't it wait until we come again?"

So he snubbed out his smoke and allowed it could. They had a long night ahead of them, thanks to her white lie about not being able to make it home, so he'd get everything she knew about Senator Fraser and his associates out of her, if she didn't screw him to death before morning.

Chapter 16

Nobody at his own office asked who Longarm had spent the night with when he showed up on time for a change. Marshal Vail sent the two notes off to be compared by that college professor he knew. Meanwhile Longarm went over Henry's typed-up transcript of his handwritten report on that useless Texas trip.

Things sure read different neatly typed in monotonous squinty letters. But things got downright ridiculous when he got to meeting up with Morgan Durante in Waco.

He rejoined Henry in the reception room and hooked a rump over a corner of the desk to wave the papers in the clerk's face, saying, "No offense, Henry, but you left a whole shooting out of this here report. Anyone just reading this would assume I'd met that Pinkerton man on my way to board a train, compared notes with him, and parted friendly. How come?"

The pasty-faced clerk said innocently, "Marshal Vail's orders. Washington gets a carbon of your official signed report. How would it look if you were to say right out you'd witnessed a killing and gone on to catch a train without a word to the local authorities?"

"Like I was in a hurry," Longarm replied, getting back to his feet as he grumbled, "I'd just as soon not write these damned fool reports to begin with. Seems to me that once I do they ought to be filed in my own words."

Without waiting for Henry's pasty-faced answer Longarm strode on back to Billy Vail's office, rapped once, and went on in without waiting for an invite. Vail asked him what he was sore about now.

When Longarm told him, the older lawman patiently explained he'd followed the drift of those rough notes—as he described a lot of serious thought—and added, "You did right to go on that way, once you saw the shooter had lit out and the shootee had been a wanted man those Waco lawmen wouldn't have wanted to share any bounty on. But these things have to be worded delicate, old son. When no harm has been done, why put it in a report for some asshole from the opposition party to get all het up about?"

Longarm grimaced and said, "You're the boss. But I ain't fixing to sign any report I never wrote, Billy."

Vail said expansively, "That's all right. Nobody in Washington would know your handwriting from Henry's, and he'd sign his own death warrant if I told him to."

Longarm smiled thinly and allowed it was no skin off his nose. But by the time he'd rejoined their clerk he was inspired to ask, "How long have you been typing that way, Henry? I mean, with some of the letters big and the others little?"

Henry glanced down at his big square machine uncertainly as he replied, "Since we got this more modern model, a couple of years ago. Don't you remember how that first Remington-Sholes we had only typed in manifold?"

Longarm squinted his eyes thoughtfully and asked, "Is manifold where you type in all capital letters, the way Western Union still does?"

Henry nodded and said, "Yes. Same reason. You need this shift key on the newer models to type in upper- and lowercase. I suppose they save time sending telegraph messages in manifold. Why are we having this conversation, by the way?"

Longarm said, "Those old war records they dug out of the files for us ain't as old as I thought. No records were typed in any style at the time because you couldn't buy typewriters until after the war."

Henry nodded and said, "Everyone knows that. But I wish I had a nickel for every page of handwritten reports I've retyped since I took this tedious job. Of course those regimental musters and old battle reports were typed up on uniform sheets to be refiled in an orderly manner, Custis. Have you any idea what a mess the originals would have been in, thrown helter-skelter together in any handy box?"

Longarm said, "Nope. I never got to *see* 'em. But let's say someone as neat as you ordered the papers of the Colorado Firsters neatly retyped and baled with that red tape—say six months after the war?"

Henry shook his head and replied, "Say nine. Minimum. Sholes got his first patents in the late '60s. But he didn't get Remington Arms to manufacture and market the first practical machines until '74."

"Which means everything typed before was typed in manifold," said Longarm. "Meaning the files I've been shown have been retyped a second time after 1874!"

Henry whistled softly and said, "You're right. But look at it the army way. Doesn't the army polish brass, whitewash rocks, and dig holes in the ground for no important reasons at all?"

Longarm nodded. "I still want a look at the doubtless dusty original handwriting. Two reasons. That letter writer may have read some sloppy handwriting wrong. Or some enemy left over from a mighty long time ago could have *written* some of those old records in the same handwriting."

He handed Billy Vail's version of his trip to Texas to Henry as he said, "The boss says you're to sign my name to these fibs. I'll be out to Camp Weld reading should anyone ask for me."

But before he could leave, the deputy who'd been sent with those two handwritten notes came back, saying, "The prof wasn't home, Henry. You want to take these papers in for me?"

Longarm grabbed them instead and headed back to Vail's office with them, muttering about paper cuts. He told Vail, "I have to get this love letter from the Widow Dunbar back up the hill, Billy. I promised another lady I'd have it back for her before her own boss missed it."

Vail shook his bullet head but said, "We can have it photographed down the hall and still get it back by noon. Will that do it?"

Longarm nodded and explained, "His secretary says he sleeps late when he hasn't anything to say on the senate floor. He don't today, and I happen to know he had a good time last night."

As Longarm handed the love letter over, another thought struck him. So he said, "They finished up that silver bill, you know, with the senator's side winning and nothing crooked about it as far as I can see."

Vail nodded. "Senator Fraser's been no worse and a lot better than some we've elected in this state. We know his secret enemy is a crook by definition. It wasn't Senator Fraser who killed that Pink protecting him and tried to kill you as you were trying to find out where those letters were coming from, right?"

Longarm agreed that was about the size of it, and went out for an early lunch at the nearby Parthenon while they had that love letter photographed and sepia-printed. So it wasn't much past eleven by the time he was striding up the steps of the State House again with a clear conscience and a slight erection inspired by pickled pigs feet, deviled eggs, and memories of a shapely figure in that hotel mirror.

163

But he was alert enough to spot a familiar but out-of-place figure just in time, and duck into a shadowy niche between two marble pillars as the squat cuss he knew as Morgan Durante scuttled by in what seemed a hurry. Then Longarm hurried on to the office door the Pink had come out of. As Una glanced up to smile in a mighty sweet way, Longarm handed her the love letter, asking, "What did Durante want with the senator, honey?"

Una looked blank, then said, "Durante? Wasn't that the name of the detective stabbed in the visitors' gallery, Custis?"

Longarm said, "It was. Morgan Durante was his brother. That was him I just saw leaving."

Una shook her head and replied, "You must be mistaken, dear. He said his name was Marner and that he was a lawyer representing some silver mining company who—"

"Which way did you send him?" Longarm asked.

Una dimpled up at him. "My heavens, you're so smart as well as virile, darling. As a matter of fact I *did* tell him Senator Fraser would probably be at his club, the Harvard Alumni on Glenarm Place, where so many members of the bar . . ."

Then Longarm was on his way. He was out the Colfax exit by the time he had the senator's home away from home located in his own head. Glenarm Place was around a quarter mile off, downhill part of the way. So he started loping down Colfax, peering ahead for some sign of a shorter, squatter cuss—moving slower, he hoped.

The mysterious Pink was nowhere in sight, and you could see a good ways down a broad avenue with open grassy slopes along one side of it.

"The son of a bitch had a pony or carriage waiting!" Longarm decided as he picked up the pace despite the odd looks he seemed to be getting from all sides.

It was a damned-if-you-do-and-damned-if-you-don't situation. He figured he could leg the five or six city blocks in the time an empty cab was apt to come along, and he was right. He almost got run down by a brewery dray on Broadway, and had a close call with a speeding coach crossing Court Place. But then he was tearing up the steps of the fancy private club, where a snooty old bird in a cutaway coat tried to stop him in the foyer with some bull about members and their damned old guests.

Longarm said, "I'm the law. Federal. Where's Senator Fraser, and did a short stout cuss in rusty black just get past you some damned way?"

The club steward smiled in a lofty way and said, "That would have been Mister Marner, another member of the bar who had an appointment here with Senator Fraser. I believe you'll find them both downstairs in the swimming pool or possibly the steam room."

Longarm was on his way, drawing his six-gun as he tore down the white marble stairs to the white-tiled basement. He busted through swinging doors, and almost fell in a big swimming pool full of naked gents. Some of them screamed like naked ladies as he waved his gun at them, demanding to know which way the steam room might be.

Once he knew where he was going, he went, tearing into a white wall of hot steam that billowed out at him as he opened the door and shouted, "Don't do it! We got every exit covered and you'll never get paid for the job either way!"

Then a shot rang out and Longarm was flat on the wet tiles with the door swinging shut behind him, aiming his .44-40 at nothing much as he just lay low to wait on what might happen next.

What happened next was a familiar voice called out through the steam, "Is that Deputy Long I just heard?"

Longarm bounced his voice off the tiles just in case as he called back, "Yep. Who fired that shot, Senator Fraser?"

The older man replied, "Me! You warned me to keep my own gun close at hand, and I suppose he never figured on that. Who *was* this, by the way? It's hard to tell amid all this steam, but I never saw the idiot before he was suddenly looming in the fog with his own gun out!"

Longarm rose, aware of how wet his suit was all down the front, as he he moved in for a better look, saying, "Down Texas way he told me his name was Durante. Said he was the brother of that real Pink murdered up in the State House. Must have had balls of solid brass. Counted on some resemblance to another real Pink who'd be away from his own branch office when a fool federal man checked by wire and bought it!"

Someone from outside had propped the door open by this time. So the steam was lifting and Longarm could see the senator, wrapped in white linen like a real Roman senator, standing over the prone form of the black-clad Durante, Marner, or rose by any other name. The senator had his own Navy Colt down at his side as they were joined by a uniformed roundsman from the Denver P.D. It saved needless explanations, but the copper badge still got it wrong when he first recognized Longarm and cheerfully asked, "Who'd you gun this time, Longarm?"

The taller federal lawman shook his head and said, "I cannot tell a lie. It was the senator here. All I know about the one bleeding all over them wet white tiles is that he once gunned a confederate of his own down in Waco to convince me he was on my side."

The senator asked why Longarm thought that. Longarm shrugged and said, "Only way it works. He sure as shit wasn't the *real* Morgan Durante. He was tracking me with his underlings down Texas way, with orders to stop me before I could find something out. They lost track of me for a spell. That meant I could have found something out and, worse yet, wired to my boss about it. So this ruthless cuss sacrificed one of his own boys to gain my confidence, learn I was still dumb as ever, and light out to report to his own boss for further instructions."

The senator stared soberly down at the body at his bare feet to say, "I guess we know now what those instructions must have *been!*"

Longarm took a deep breath, let half of it out lest his voice crack, and calmly suggested, "Nope. You gunned him before I could even guess. So why don't you tell us what they would have been and—"

They both fired at the same time.

Longarm had figured that might happen. So he'd naturally sidestepped as he brought his own gun up to match the older man's last desperate try. The senator's .36–30 round played hob with a wall tile across the steam room as he took Longarm's .44–40 slug just over the heart to slam back against the wet tiles on behind him and slide slowly down to the floor, dropping his weapon and losing his linen toga along the way as he stared blankly up at them through slowly clearing steam and gunsmoke without saying a word.

The copper badge broke the long stunned silence with: "Jesus H. Christ! You just gunned a state senator, Longarm! I'll back your word he was out to gun you too. But *why,* in the name of Our Lord?"

Longarm said, "I'm still working on it. But I suspect names had a lot to do with it. To begin with I knew the dead man in the black duds never would have got in upstairs so easy if this here member in his birthday suit hadn't told that snip at the front door he was expecting a guest. I don't know which one of 'em murdered the real Durante. I can work it either way, now that I know there's a side exit to the stairs from the senator's private office."

By this time other club members had crowded in to join them. So Federal Judge Dickerson of the Denver District Court was listening, in his own Roman toga, as the copper badge demanded, "How come Senator Fraser shot his pal, instead of *you,* if they were plotting things together?"

Longarm ejected the spent brass and reloaded as he sighed and replied, "Same reason his head gunslick sacrificed a black woolly lamb down in Waco. He knew I was on to the fake Pinkerton man, but he wanted to know whether I was on to *him*. You saw what happened when he saw I was."

Judge Dickerson proved an elderly gent with skinny bare legs could still look imposing as he declared, "It's a good thing you've appeared before me on wilder charges and seem to have an eyewitness to back you this time, Deputy Long. But you've still made awfully wild charges against a respected member of the bar, young sir, and I'd certainly like to hear more details!"

Longarm put his gun away as he soberly replied, "So would I, Your Honor. With your permission, I'd like to leave Curtis here in charge of these bodies so I can question others before they get word of this mysterious mess!"

The half-naked judge nodded sternly and said, "I can promise you nobody outside this club will hear about it before sundown. Do you think you'll need more time than that?"

Longarm said, "Not if I'm guessing right about the way some dots might connect after all. There ain't enough time in eternity if I'm still guessing wrong!"

Chapter 17

Longarm found he could get around faster on a borrowed police mount with his federal badge pinned to a lapel. But it was still after four that afternoon when he made his last stop at the Fraser house up on Capitol Hill.

He dismounted, tethered the lathered bay gelding to the hitching post out front, and took the sandstone steps two at a time. A guardsman who'd been seated on the porch rail popped to port arms, but didn't try to stop a visitor he recognized as a federal lawman. Longarm just told the prissy butler to get the hell out of his way as he let himself in, and strode for that study where, sure enough, he found Elsbeth Fraser holding court over some slightly younger society gals.

When the rather grand Elsbeth chided him for not waiting to be announced, Longarm said, "I'm running late. But I see I got here in time. You other ladies will have to excuse us. Miss Elsbeth and me have some serious secrets to share."

When the other three old bats exchanged glances without moving Longarm snapped, "I meant right now! What are you all waiting for, some good-bye kissing?"

That got them going. As the last one tore out, the senator's spinster sister rose imperiously to warn him,

"You had no right to speak to my guests, or any ladies, like that!"

He replied, not unkindly, "I didn't think you wanted 'em sharing family secrets, ma'am. I'm hoping to get out of here without making any arrests. But you gotta admit you and your brother have both done some mighty silly things in your time."

Her face went ashen, but her expression never changed as she cautiously sank back to her sofa, asking, "Whatever are you talking about, Custis?"

Longarm remained on his feet, covering the doorway along with her as he replied, "I've been talking a blue streak with heaps of folks ever since I left your brother's club with a better handle on who I wanted to talk to. Would you mind if I smoked, ma'am? To tell the truth, I ain't had the chance for some time."

She nodded, and he fished out a cheroot as he continued. "I rode first to Camp Weld, where a helpful but otherwise useless Colorado Guard clerk gave me directions to the archives I was looking for back in downtown Denver. Then I fought my way through red tape and cobwebs to the original records of Chivington's Four Hundred as of 1862. It wasn't as tough as I'd feared because only a year or more back somebody on the governor's commission for veterans' affairs had ordered 'em dug out and typed up—to make 'em easier to read, he said."

The older woman must have been feeling sick as hell by this time, but she just nodded and said, "My brother mentioned someone from his campaign committee doing that. He was always modest about what he described in his humorous way as his service in the chorus of that comic opera. But his friends felt his combat record would give him the edge he needed in a contest with a Quaker who sat the war out. Our county over in the Front Range was mostly settled by veterans who rated extra points on their claims, and so—"

"Miss Una Gordon explained all that to me at the office," Longarm said, with a thoughtful glance at the fading light outside as he continued. "It might save time if I told you how an earlier conversation with our own clerk-typist inspired me to wonder how far a twice-typed transcript might stray from the original handwriting. You've known all along your brother was never anywhere near that fighting around Glorieta Pass. So let's get to those wild accusations about him murdering rebel scouts who were never murdered."

She said, "You'd have to take my brother's military records up with *him*. I've no idea what you're talking about!"

Longarm had a good poker face as well. He nodded curtly and told her, "I ain't sure inflated war records are a federal offense. I sure hope they ain't. But exposing him as a bare-faced liar would surely hurt him politically. So let's talk about whether you were out to bust him up with the voters or just that pretty young Fionna Dunbar. You were mighty sneaky with those European handwriting mistakes, and just as you hoped, a government handwriting expert would have been willing to testify no native-born American had made 'em!"

He got ready to grab her imposing weight if she fainted. But she only went sort of green around the gills as she demanded he stop playing cat and mouse and get to the damned point.

He nodded and said, "I've been to see both Kate Thayer and the pretty Widow Dunbar this afternoon. I asked some trick questions, and unless both ladies deserve to be on the stage as really famous actress gals, neither has what we call the guilty knowledge needed to write those threatening letters in any sort of handwriting. Kate Thayer was still in school and Fionna Dunbar was in Scotland during the Battle of Glorieta."

Elsbeth Fraser demanded in a lofty tone, "Are you suggesting *I* was there, Custis?"

171

He smiled thinly at the picture and replied, "Not hardly. You was here in Denver, albeit at a less fancy address, whilst keeping the home fires burning for your more adventurous baby brother."

He moved over to a glass-fronted bookcase as he continued. "I know *none* of you logical suspects could have been there when that lost patrol was massacred by a Union lance corporal because nothing like that ever happened. The only postwar book that even puts those particular names in any patrol, erroneously, only *speculates* on what might have happened to them."

He pointed at the bookcase with his chin. "I see you have a copy of those Confederate speculations on Glorieta, along with heaps of other war books, ma'am."

She replied in a desperately casual tone, "Those are my brother's books. As a veteran he naturally takes more interest in old military matters than I."

Longarm said in an amiable tone, "I'm sure that's true most of the time, ma'am. But a letter writer who was never anywhere near the Battle of Glorieta would naturally have to look things up, and this fine library of old war books would have held all such a sneak might ever need, including the names of men who died on both sides."

She started to say something about that. But Longarm hushed her with a gentle wave of his cheroot. "I just proved how suddenly one can get from here to Texas, and nobody was watching you when those first letters were posted out of town. Your brother was up in the mountains, kissing voters' babies when he wasn't kissing the Widow Dunbar, who'd tagged along. Kate Thayer can prove where *she* was at the time, thanks to a busy social life and a pest called Jefferson Pryce who keeps trying to get her to hold hands with him."

She snapped, "That doesn't prove *I* went anywhere!"

To which he gently replied, "We don't have to. You proved you'd been sending 'em when you sent that last one from inside this very house. Before you say you never

172

did, it just won't work any better way. There was a state trooper on the far side of the door in broad day when you say yourself your butler found the letter in your box *inside* the door. We call what happens next the process of elimination, ma'am. A mighty spry sneak could have found it *possible* to sneak a message past a sentry on duty. But why would anyone take such a chance when there's a letter box on most every corner out front?"

She tried, "It must have been Beverly then! He's one of those men who like other men, and perhaps he was jealous of my brother's infatuation with that jumped-up Lowland tart."

Longarm had a time meeting her wide-eyed stare as he quietly told her, "We both know who was driven crazy jealous when the only man she'd ever slept with left her old and fat for a younger gal he really meant to marry up with after all those years as a bachelor, living at home with an unmarried kinswoman."

She fell to her knees on the rug, covering her scarlet face with her pudgy fingers as she sobbed, "Stop it! Not another word! I'll confess to writing those silly letters if you'll promise you won't let on to Jay-Jay that you've even suspected our silly but harmless family secrets! It would kill him if he thought anyone knew!"

Longarm assured her quietly, "Just clear that letter writing up for us and you have my word your brother will never hear a word of what you have to tell us, ma'am."

Chapter 18

She did. As she was dictating her full pathetic confession to Billy Vail and Henry, Longarm left before anyone had to tell her where her baby brother lay at the moment. On his way out, Longarm mentioned his having to return a horse to the Denver P.D. But when he got out front, he mounted the bay tethered next to Elsbeth Fraser's carriage team, told her driver his mistress would be inside a while, and rode another way entirely.

The western sky was red and gold above the purple Front Range as Longarm crested Capitol Hill to the east again. Kate Thayer was almost as rich but not as fancy. So it was her in the flesh coming out on her shady porch as he tethered the police mount out front.

As he moved up the sandstone walk she smiled down at him to say, "I was just about to fix supper and I've enough for the two of us if you don't mind roughing it. I'm afraid I gave my servants the night off, Custis."

He knew most quality folks gave their help a weekday off instead of Saturday or Sunday, when they were more inclined to entertain. So he just said, "I reckon my pony and me have the time, if you've fodder and water for him as well, Miss Kate."

She nodded approvingly, and told him to just lead his

police mount around the back to her stable while she put the kettle on.

He did. He saw she'd let her household help borrow her own rig and carriage team. He figured she rode the paint cow pony in the end stall personally. He unsaddled the bay, and led it into the next stall before he unbridled it to leave it content with fodder and water.

As he recrossed the backyard Kate Thayer waved him in through her kitchen door. He hung his hat up and took the seat she waved him to at her pine table. He admired a rich gal who was enough of a sport to put an apron on over her calico summer frock and pitch in. As she was busting eggs into an earthenware bowl, Kate reminded him he'd promised to come back and tell her what he'd found out as soon as he'd questioned those other suspects.

He said, "Aw, you were never much of a suspect, ma'am, and the Widow Dunbar was as innocent, save for some slap and tickle with a gent who should have been ashamed of his fool self. Elsbeth Fraser was the one who wrote them crazy letters. She was trying to get a wayward baby brother to come back home by costing him his job while inspiring him to think another lady with more European handwriting had done it."

Kate turned to face him with an astounded look, brushing a wisp of oak-leaf hair from her brow with the back of one wrist as she demanded, "The poor senator's own sister was sending those vicious accusations and death threats, Custis? I can't believe it! Why would any loving sister do a thing like that?"

He looked awkwardly away as he muttered, "Let's just say there's sisterly loving and then there's other sorts of loving. It ain't the sort of story for mixed company, Miss Kate."

She said, "I'm a big girl now. I breed my own stock and, damn it, you're talking about a man who's been handling my money!"

He nodded soberly and said, "Honestly, as far as we

175

can tell. He served his county well in the state senate too. But he did have a few skeletons in his closet—aside from Miss Elsbeth, I mean—and what are we having for supper, scrambled eggs?"

She sniffed, "I'm making us a soufflé and it's going to take a while to rise. Are you accusing my guardian and his sister of incest, Custis?"

He shrugged and said, "It happens. She's down at my office and they're taking it all down. But I doubt my boss will press federal charges. The poor old gal has enough on her plate, once it comes to her how her nasty notes got so many others killed."

Kate Thayer shoved her mysterious makings in her oven, and came over to the table to take a seat across from him as she told him, "We won't be eating for at least forty-five minutes. So I want you to just start at the beginning and remember what I said about being a big girl now, Custis."

He got out a cheroot and held it up for her to nod or shake her head. When she nodded he lit up, enjoyed a thoughtful drag as he gathered his thoughts, and began. "Once upon a time there was a ripsnorting younger Denver inhabited by settlers from all over. So when that war broke out back East, some favored one side whilst others chose different."

She nodded soberly and said, "I was here, old enough to read the papers, Custis."

He said, "I know. So were the Frasers. Don't horn in unless you've something to say I don't already know. What neither you nor your own Union folks knew was that your dad's lawyer, J.J. Fraser, for reasons one can only guess at now, left his older sister here in Denver to watch their then-modest property as he ran off to Texas to join up with Sibley's Brigade."

Kate gasped. "Uncle Jay-Jay a rebel raider? Surely you jest!"

He shook his head. "We got the whole story out of

his sister just now. She was singing like a bird about less disgusting family secrets in hopes we might not ask whose notion it was to stay home nights a lot."

Kate still looked unconvinced as he looked about for some place to flick ashes, saying, "A share of the loot and a position with the Confederate government of Colorado may have served as his motive at the time. A rider who already knew the lay of the land up this way would have rated at least a few stripes from the other side. The two-faced rascal's sister thinks he led a squad of scouts. So it ain't impossible Fraser himself led that lost patrol another vet of the half-baked campaign got all wrong in his own memoirs!"

She rose from the table to fetch him an ashtray as he went on. "Whether he and his pals deserted then or later, he deserted as soon as he saw who was winning and simply made his way back home to his Denver mailing address. His sister had been keeping house all the while, and naturally fibbing to any neighbors who inquired after Lawyer Fraser of Denver. In the meanwhile lots of gents up Colorado way, such as your own dad, had joined the three regiments of Colorado Volunteers. So Fraser joined up too."

Kate Thayer proved she was an old soldier's daughter by asking Longarm, "*After* the Battle of Glorieta, you mean?"

Longarm flicked some tobacco ash in her kindly provided tray and replied, "Yep. But it was only a few weeks after, and few vets have call to question any enlistment dates but their own. I don't think Fraser was out to fool anyone at the time. He just wanted to prove he was a patriot on the winning side. Serving a few weekends out at Camp Weld would have left him forever fixed in the uncertain memories of other part-time soldiers blue. After the war, joining the G.A.R. and other veterans' groups, the senator, like many another veteran, likely improved his war record a tad. It ain't hard. I meet lots of old boys who say they were at Shiloh with me, on one side or another, and unless they make bodacious mistakes, I just can't tell whether or not they were on some other part of the field there."

"But the written records . . ."

"Who looks when it's just a saloon brag? I just heard from Miss Elsbeth how the senator himself never wanted his political pals bragging on his brags in print. But once they got him elected as a veteran of the only battle the Colorado Volunteers would like to be remembered for, he was stuck with his fibs and doubtless sweating bullets about 'em until he managed, as the state governor's adviser on the state guard, to order a heap of sloppy old records transcribed on a spanking-new Remington Manifold in his own office suite. Would you care to guess who typed up just one or two substitute pages, doubtless after hours?"

Kate dimpled across the table at him to declare, "Even I can see how easy that would be to manage. But why didn't he destroy . . . Oh, I see. The originals would have to be repacked and returned to the old files, even though nobody would ever want to bother with them?"

He nodded and said, "He had them updated in more modern type just a year ago to make the trail back longer. Then he did slip just one regimental muster out of the old handwritten files. I found the box easier as a result. He should have taken his chances with the sloppy original mess. The more recent typing, transcribed from the manifold, had been done innocently enough by a company clerk. But you know what they say about a guilty conscience making one act guilty."

She rose to fetch cups, saucers, and tea kettle as she told him she never did anything that made her feel guilty. So he went on. "It's just as well for me it was him, not you, going loco when those letters started coming, accusing him of all sorts of things he knew he couldn't have done. He never guessed they were pathetic attempts to bust him up with the Widow Dunbar and inspire him to fort up with

178

the only gal who knew all his secrets."

Kate demurely asked whether they were talking about the dirty old man's war record or sex life. So Longarm said, "Both. She had a way of warming up in the privacy of their own home. But forget what *she* did and let's talk about what *he* did once she'd done it."

Kate poured tea, asking if he could hold out on more solid grub till her fancy soufflé rose to the occasion. He allowed that he could, and snubbed out his smoke to sip politely as he continued. "The senator had to respond in some way to the charges and death threats, knowing how many others knew about 'em. He asked for federal help instead of the local help more likely to have old state militia records handy in unexpected places. You and me together scared him some more when we failed to play our parts as planned in his charade. You went and hired that Pinkerton man. Dave Durante was a good detective with a rep for taking nothing for granted. Like a fool I ignored his routine investigative procedure. I was in a hurry, and it just never occurred to me a state senator would send threatening letters to himself."

She nodded soberly and said, "You were right, Custis. He naturally never accused himself of crimes he'd never committed!"

Longarm said, "Let's stick to the crimes he did commit. Durante wanted a routine investigation, digging into all the details of everybody's dirty linen. The senator was more worried about his own dirty linen than anything a good Pink and his agency might find out about crank letter writers. Allan Pinkerton put the U.S. Secret Service together for Abe Lincoln during the war. So Lord only knows what sort of old records, Union or Confederate, a determined Pinkerton man could get into if he really put his mind to it!"

"Then that's why poor Detective Durante was murdered!" she gasped.

It had been a statement rather than a question. But

Longarm nodded and said, "By the senator himself, or mayhaps by one of the old Texas gunslicks he recruited fast as soon as he felt threatened. It's too early to say whether he knew the head gunslinger of old or might have just recruited him through mutual friends. Save for a little incest and a spotty war record, the senator seems to have tried to be an honest lawyer and decent enough party man."

He held a hand over his cup as she tried to pour cream in it, and when she gave that sissy notion up he continued. "Be that as it may. The killings might have ended there if I'd just run in circles here in Denver. The senator had done nothing to inspire anyone to dig into Confederate records in West Texas. But those Texas postmarks on the earlier letters sent me on a wild-goose chase. Neither the senator nor me had any notion Miss Elsbeth had cribbed her accusation from a very poor account of the campaign, written by an imaginative hack who hadn't known what he was doing. So I tore off to Texas after evidence that wasn't there, and the senator, not knowing what I might find, had his gun slicks go after me to prevent me from finding anything, see?"

She wrinkled her pert nose and replied, "I see what you mean about a guilty conscience. Didn't you find it all very confusing?"

He chuckled dryly and said, "I sure did. So did they. I lucked out a few times and threw them off my trail a spell. Next time they had me pegged they knew I'd had plenty of time to find out almost anything and, worse yet, wire it to my boss. You see, they had no more idea than I did who was sending those fool letters, based on what they didn't know. So once they caught up with me in Waco, their boss gun sacrificed one of his own to get in good with me, and I, still in the dark as I tried to connect dots that refused to connect in any sensible way, fell for that simple ploy like a chump!"

She reached across the table to pat the back of his wrist

MANITOUWADGE PUBLIC LIBRARY

in a comforting way as she said, "I don't think you were a chump, Custis. You were only thinking like a human being when that ruthless villain murdered his own friend just to strike up a friendly conversation!"

He remained unconvinced as he mused, half to himself, "Wonder if that fake Pink killed Blacky's younger side-kick or not. Oh, well, suffice it to say it failed to fool me a second time when the senator gunned his boss gun in that steam room downtown. I forgot to tell you earlier today how I wound up shooting it out with the cornered rat. But it ain't a pretty story for the supper table. So suffice it to say a heap of dots got connected in an unexpected pattern when it suddenly hit me that the hired gun I was saving the senator from had gotten into a private club as the senator's invited guest. I've already told Miss Elsbeth how an otherwise impossible mail delivery made a mighty obvious dot of her, and once I'd talked to you, Widow Dunbar, and some file clerks out at Camp Weld I sure felt stupid. So let's just eat that mighty swell egg shuffle I smell and say no more about it."

They did. It seemed to take no more than a tiny slice of eternity before even her peach cobbler dessert was gone and it was downright dark outside. So he felt obliged to say it was getting time for him to get it on down the road.

But then she was holding hands with him across the table as she gasped, "Oh, no, Custis! All my servants are away for the night, and didn't you say one of the gang is still at large?"

He started to assure her that the shabby Texican gun slick was likely running for home, if not the border, if he was still alive. But then he wondered why any man would want to say anything as dumb as that. So he just went on holding hands with her as he allowed he could stay and protect her all night, if that was what she really wanted.

181

Watch for

LONGARM AND THE DEAD RINGERS

180th in the bold LONGARM series
from Jove

Coming in December!

If you enjoyed this book, subscribe now and get...

TWO FREE

A $7.00 VALUE—

If you would like to read more of the very best, most exciting, adventurous, action-packed Westerns being published today, you'll want to subscribe to True Value's Western Home Subscription Service.

Each month the editors of True Value will select the 6 very best Westerns from America's leading publishers for special readers like you. You'll be able to preview these new titles as soon as they are published, *FREE* for ten days with no obligation!

TWO FREE BOOKS

When you subscribe, we'll send you your first month's shipment of the newest and best 6 Westerns for you to preview. With your first shipment, two of these books will be yours as our introductory gift to you absolutely *FREE* (a $7.00 value), regardless of what you decide to do. If you like them, as much as we think you will, keep all six books but pay for just 4 at the low subscriber rate of just $2.75 each. If you decide to return them, keep 2 of the titles as our gift. No obligation.

Special Subscriber Savings

When you become a True Value subscriber you'll save money several ways. First, all regular monthly selections will be billed at the low subscriber price of just $2.75 each. That's at least a savings of $4.50 each month below the publishers price. Second, there is never any shipping, handling or other hidden charges—*Free home delivery*. What's more there is no minimum number of books you must buy, you may return any selection for full credit and you can cancel your subscription at any time. A TRUE VALUE!

A special offer for people who enjoy reading the best Westerns published today.

WESTERNS!

NO OBLIGATION

Mail the coupon below

To start your subscription and receive 2 FREE WESTERNS, fill out the coupon below and mail it today. We'll send your first shipment which includes 2 FREE BOOKS as soon as we receive it.

Mail To: **True Value Home Subscription Services, Inc. P.O. Box 5235
120 Brighton Road, Clifton, New Jersey 07015-5235**

YES! I want to start reviewing the very best Westerns being published today. Send me my first shipment of 6 Westerns for me to preview FREE for 10 days. If I decide to keep them, I'll pay for just 4 of the books at the low subscriber price of $2.75 each; a total $11.00 (a $21.00 value). Then each month I'll receive the 6 newest and best Westerns to preview Free for 10 days. If I'm not satisfied I may return them within 10 days and owe nothing. Otherwise I'll be billed at the special low subscriber rate of $2.75 each; a total of $16.50 (at least a $21.00 value) and save $4.50 off the publishers price. There are never any shipping, handling or other hidden charges. I understand I am under no obligation to purchase any number of books and I can cancel my subscription at any time, no questions asked. In any case the 2 FREE books are mine to keep.

Name _____

Street Address _____ Apt. No. _____

City _____ State _____ Zip Code _____

Telephone _____

Signature _____
(if under 18 parent or guardian must sign)

Terms and prices subject to change. Orders subject
to acceptance by True Value Home Subscription
Services, Inc.

11238-0

LONGARM

Explore the exciting Old West with one of the men who made it wild!

___LONGARM AND THE LONE STAR CAPTIVE   0-515-10646-1/$4.50
(Giant novel)
___LONGARM #1   0-515-08965-6/$3.99
___LONGARM AND THE FOOL KILLER #167   0-515-10980-0/$3.99
___LONGARM AND THE SHOSHONI SILVER #168 0-515-10997-5/$3.99
___LONGARM AND THE NIGHT BRANDERS #169 0-515-11018-3/$3.99
___LONGARM AND THE TAOS TERROR #170   0-515-11043-4/$3.99
___LONGARM AND THE NEVADA SWINDLE #171 0-515-11061-2/$3.99
___LONGARM ON THE BUTTERFIELD SPUR #172 0-515-11082-5/$3.99
___LONGARM AND THE DIAMOND   0-515-11103-1/$3.99
   SNATCHERS #173
___LONGARM AND THE BORDER SHOWDOWN   0-515-11119-8/$3.99
   #174
___LONGARM AND THE CARNIVAL KILLER #175 0-515-11136-8/$3.99
___LONGARM AND THE CAPTIVE WOMEN #176   0-515-11166-X/$3.99
___LONGARM AND THE NAVAHO DRUMS   0-515-11164-3/$4.50
(Giant novel)
___LONGARM IN THE CROSS FIRE #177   0-515-11194-5/$3.99
___LONGARM AND THE GOLDEN DEATH #178   0-515-11216-X/$3.99
___LONGARM AND THE REBEL'S REVENGE #179 0-515-11238-0/$3.99
___LONGARM AND THE DEAD RINGERS #180   0-515-11255-0/$3.99
(December)
___LONGARM AND THE BOUNTY   0-515-11283-6/$3.99
   OF BLOOD #181   (January 1994)

For Visa, MasterCard and American Express orders ($15 minimum) call: 1-800-631-8571

FOR MAIL ORDERS: CHECK BOOK(S). FILL
OUT COUPON. SEND TO:

BERKLEY PUBLISHING GROUP
390 Murray Hill Pkwy., Dept. B
East Rutherford, NJ 07073

NAME _____

ADDRESS _____

CITY _____

STATE _____ ZIP _____

PLEASE ALLOW 6 WEEKS FOR DELIVERY.
PRICES ARE SUBJECT TO CHANGE WITHOUT NOTICE.

POSTAGE AND HANDLING:
$1.75 for one book, 75¢ for each
additional. Do not exceed $5.50.

BOOK TOTAL $ _____

POSTAGE & HANDLING $ _____

APPLICABLE SALES TAX $ _____
(CA, NJ, NY, PA)

TOTAL AMOUNT DUE $ _____

PAYABLE IN US FUNDS.
(No cash orders accepted.)

201e